Slam

THE RILEY BROTHERS BOOK 5

E. DAVIES

Slam / E. Davies. – 2nd ed.
ISBN: 978-1-912245-04-8

CHAPTER

One

KEVIN

"Push yourself, Kevin. You can't get back fast enough, you'll get better at that."

Kevin was sweating as he pushed himself back from the board to skate backwards across the ice again, avoiding CJ. He kept his eyes sweeping back and forth as if to check for pucks.

Cam had been right, goddamn it. Kevin had to move faster backwards if he wanted to have any offensive depth. He was still too defensive to make the really ballsy passes that he'd have to make if he made the first line someday.

But that was why he'd hired Glenn, one of the top private trainers in the city. The gap in knowledge and skill level between his university level and the minor leagues was huge. Now, he was just one step below one of the oldest teams in Canadian hockey league history.

It wasn't a team most guys wanted to play for, but it was one of the closest teams to his hometown back in New Brunswick, at least. He'd be able to get home more often than if he got signed in California or something ridiculous.

"Good!" Glenn called as Kevin reached the starting point again. "Hey, CJ, what do you call that? Go do it again."

Kevin took a moment to push his hair back, the sweat cooling on his skin under his jersey and practice padding. The cold arena air was what he lived and breathed; he much preferred it to sticky Toronto summers. Being acclimatized to it cost him a fortune, because he had to keep the A/C turned way down. Otherwise, he spent all his time at home lying on his bed or the couch complaining about the heat to his roommate.

Hans ignored most of his complaints. He had a lot of stories about how hot it got in his German hometown. Kevin suspected most of them were bullshit from his rudimentary Google searches, but he never called the guy out on it.

"Damn," Kevin whistled at the speed of CJ's rebound. The guy was insanely quick.

"Okay, boys. Your ice time will run out in a couple minutes, so get your asses moving. One more drill to do."

"Yes, sir," Kevin saluted with two fingers. He was splitting the ice rental with three other guys Glenn trained. They all wanted a little ice time, and Glenn agreed so he could judge how much they'd improved this month.

Kevin was probably in the best position of all of them. He hadn't played a full season on his university team, and he hadn't been dragged through the playoffs. And compared to the wear and tear of the major leagues, not to mention the stress and pressure, what he'd experienced before was nothing.

He could see the toll it took on everyone: the first couple weeks had been mostly pilates and yoga, stretching and limbering exercises, and a little weight loss for the guys who ate mostly chicken wings after games.

It didn't discourage him, though. As Kevin flicked a puck along his blade and took off down the ice with it, he felt that same familiar thrill run through his body. It didn't matter if he was doing this in front of a packed arena for a game or by himself on a quiet Tuesday afternoon on the lake back home.

He lived for that rush to his fingers and toes and cheeks – the one that said *I'm right here, and I'm going for it.*

CJ tried to get between him and the empty net, and it partly worked: he flicked his wrist to send the puck into the goal, but it bounced off the crossbar.

Kevin saw his chance, though – he darted around CJ, nestled the puck at the bottom of his blade, and slapped it straight into the net.

"Nice," CJ approved, punching his arm and circling back to wait for Hemmer's approach.

Kevin took a moment to pump his fist as he shifted to skate backwards towards the net and look for Glenn's reaction. Then he pushed himself away from it again, heading up the side board.

"Watch your weight distribution," Glenn told him, his arms folded tightly. His eyes were already on Hemmer, who was duking it out with CJ in the neutral zone. "Can't let someone knock you off-balance when you're about to score. I could have hit you with a feather there."

Frustration welled in Kevin's chest, but he nodded sharply. He hadn't felt solid on his feet, so Glenn was no doubt right. But it felt sometimes like he never won anything fully anymore. Even if he nailed a great move in the few practices and partial games he'd played this month, Glenn always had something else to point out.

But that was life these days. As he and Hemmer rotated in to act as defense while CJ and Fisher practiced, Kevin didn't dwell on it. If he wanted to earn his keep around here, he had to take every bit of critique on board and use it to improve himself. He couldn't let the coach criticize the same thing twice.

In the locker room once their time was up, Kevin's mind was still on that moment. Could he have stepped the other way around CJ? He couldn't very well grab CJ's stick, but he might have knocked it aside – but then he would have missed the rebound...

"Hey, Kev. You're a million miles away."

Kevin blinked and refocused on the hand obnoxiously snapping in front of his eyes as CJ slapped his arm with the other hand. He elbowed CJ in the gut and laughed, yanking his jersey off. "Sorry, I was replaying. What?"

"We're going out to a bar tonight. Cruising for the *ladies*," CJ drawled. He elbowed Kevin back, then sat on the bench to yank off his shin guards. "You in?"

Kevin hedged and threw a careless shrug out there, tossing his shoulder pads into his bag. "I dunno, man. I'm training early tomorrow." How would he explain that picking up chicks wasn't his idea of a good time without outing himself?

"Come on, you haven't felt the *pro* effect yet," Hemmer laughed.

"The what?"

CJ nodded. "When you introduce yourself as a hockey player. It works at any sports bar... or most regular bars. You can't tell me you haven't tried it." He elbowed Kevin again, but Kevin dodged and shoved him off.

Not with women, that was for sure. Kevin scoffed and zipped up his bag. "Nah, man."

"Some of us, some Leafs will all be there. A mixed crowd.

You gotta get out sometime, man! Even if you're too busy to get laid..."

Kevin laughed. "Okay, fine."

He rubbed his face, then held out a hand to grip CJ's forearm and clap his back in a quick goodbye. "See you, then. Text me when you're going out."

"Awesome," Fisher told him. "We will."

Hemmer waved. "See you, man."

"See ya." Kevin shouldered his bag and took off out of there, gripping the strap tightly. There were two equally huge risks to going out. One was that he'd get distracted by the wrong things when he had to focus so hard on his career this summer. The other...

Kevin remembered what Cam had told him Coach Walker said to him: "Keep your head down until you're ready to be the poster boy." The first out gay pro league player was going to have a wild ride.

All Kevin wanted to do was play well and go home happy with the game he'd played. Maybe with a guy, but not in front of the cameras. Maybe with a bunch of the guys, just as friends.

In any case, he had to start by making friends.

Tonight's the night.

CHAPTER
Two

MATTY

"THE ONLY GUY WORSE FOR IT IS *THAT* ASSHOLE." FISHER'S finger jabbed Matty in the chest, jolting him out of his reverie.

Matty shoved his shoulder into Fisher's, nearly knocking the guy off his bar stool. He laughed as Fisher scrambled back onto it. "What lies are you telling now?"

"Nothing!" Fisher retorted, leaning back so Matty could see the guy on his other side. "We're telling Kevin to get out more."

Matty had seen Kevin once or twice in the gym. They'd never really talked yet. Had he noticed him, though?

Oh, hell, yeah.

The guy had gorgeous long lashes and bright eyes, an as-yet-unbroken nose, and smile lines on either side of his full lips. He was broad, but not built like a tank. He looked lean and honed even under his t-shirt.

That was another thing: he was wearing a t-shirt and dark jeans, a little more casual than the guys who were obviously dressing up to get girls tonight. They all had cologne and collared shirts on, and they were casting their eyes around the bar now and then.

Kevin, though, was just leaning against the counter, a beer bottle in one hand. He raised it and nodded slightly. "Hey."

"Hi," Matty answered, hoping Kevin hadn't noticed the once-over that he'd just given him. It was pretty normal for hockey players to size each other up, anyway. It was probably all the testosterone. He sipped his beer, then stood up and stepped around Fisher to shake hands. "How's it goin'? You're one of the new guys, aren't you?"

"Yeah, I am," Kevin laughed. "Been in town about a month."

"Training with Glenn, too, huh? Smart move," Matty told him. "I've been working with him for three years now and I get back way more than I put in."

Kevin brightened up. "Yeah? Sweet, man. Thanks."

"I've seen you working out, too. He's pushing you pretty hard. You finish a season already?"

"Yeah, I transferred from Fredericton."

Fredericton... it only took Matty a second to figure out who else he knew from there. "Oh, shit, really? Like Cam?"

Cameron had been one of his teammates before he'd been forced out of hockey from a medical condition right before being called up. In his stead, Matty had gotten the spot. Cam had been really fucking good about it, though — not jealous or snarky at all. Cam was great and low-drama. Matty missed the guy.

"Yeah, Cam Riley?" Kevin answered, grinning. "I know him. He's a good buddy of mine."

"No shit. He told me one of his friends was coming out." Matty punched Kevin's arm lightly, and... Kevin's tongue darted across his lips. Just for the briefest of seconds, before Kevin raised his bottle for another quick sip and laughed.

That was a distinct tingle of interest down Matty's spine.

Shit, however pretty the new guy was, he couldn't get turned on by him. For so many reasons.

He tried to ignore that suspicion: *if Cam's gay, is Kevin?* But no, they all had plenty of straight buddies — or buddies who said they were straight, anyway. No out gay players at the top level meant most guys were pretty quiet about it all the way down.

"Yeah?" Kevin grinned as he pushed his empty bottle across the counter and made eye contact with a bartender to ask for another. "That's awesome. Dude. Small world."

"It is, man." When Matty glanced back at Fisher, he was chatting to a blonde woman on the other side of the bar. "Oh, of course he's gone already."

Kevin laughed. "Yeah, they invited me out to pick up girls and make friends here. Apparently I'm supposed to get out of the gym more. I'm always in there."

"I know," Matty grinned. "I'm always the last one in there."

"Yeah, me too. Like I said." Kevin's chest swelled as he stood a little straighter, like he was challenging Matty.

Matty let it drop. He didn't need a contest of Biggest Gym Addict right now. He just gave an easygoing smile to help Kevin relax. "So you knew Cam in school?"

"Yeah, most of the kids in that town know each other," Kevin told him. "He was a bit older than me, but the hockey kids all know each other, believe me."

Matty knew that feeling. "I'm from a small town too." He clinked bottles with Kevin when he got his new beer and paid. "I'm sorry. I know that clique feeling."

Kevin laughed. "Yeah. Anyway, Cam got signed here pronto. I finished up my degree in Fredericton first." He said it almost apologetically.

"That's cool," Matty told him instantly. As far as Matty was concerned, he didn't have anything to apologize for. It wasn't like he was doing a PhD and still waiting to be picked, like the last kid up against the wall in dodgeball. Matty hadn't seen the guy play yet, mind, but Coach Walker wouldn't have wanted him if he didn't have talent or grit, probably both.

Kevin relaxed when Matty didn't judge him or anything, then nodded. "What about you?"

"Been here on your team a couple seasons now, and I got called up for this season."

"Oh yeah? You play forward, right?"

"Yeah. You too?"

Kevin nodded.

That explained the weird bit of defensiveness. They could be competing for the same spot on the team someday, even though it didn't really work that way. "Right, left…?" Matty asked.

"Left," Kevin told him.

Phew. Future linemates, maybe. "Centre," Matty countered with a nod. "For now, anyway. We'll see what happens after camp."

Prospects camp: their chance to prove themselves. They could get sent home, or they could get a spot on the first line. The latter was a lot less likely, but the whiz kids could earn their place at the head of the team by showing off their talents.

Matty wished he had that kind of natural spark. His hockey had always been about grinding through, not showing up with a few flashy moves and a combative attitude and expecting that to open doors. He didn't kid himself: there was a lot more competition out there than there were spots on this team, and a guy who was easy to get along with was more valuable than a princess talent.

"Ugh," Kevin shivered. "I don't know what to expect."

"It's intense, but it's good," Matty reassured him. "It's awesome. The coach is there, he doesn't take bullshit. Everyone works his ass off and the best guys stay. Good old-fashioned grit."

Whenever Kevin smiled, his face lit up; when he talked hockey, there was passion in his eyes and he leaned forward a little. His t-shirt clung to his body, moving with him rather than giving Matty a peek down at his chest.

Shit, no. Don't be a creep, Matty told himself. He had this odd feeling that Kevin wouldn't mind it, but he couldn't be sure... and he couldn't be wrong.

Kevin's energy alone was magnetic. He refused to lean in towards Kevin no matter how much as he wanted to.

"Yeah. That's why I'm training so hard this summer," Kevin admitted. "Cam told me the first season's the big one. You gotta show your potential, even if you're not there yet." His eyes were filled with that nervous energy.

"Yeah," Matty told him. "Just take it easy. It seems scary the first time, but everyone wants you to do well." Matty remembered those feelings: the nervous excitement about being given a shot to go further than he ever had, the terror that somehow he was an impostor and he'd be kicked off the team for being a shitty player, and worst of all, the sucker punch that was reading message board speculation about his potential. "And you've got the trainer of a lifetime on your side right now."

"Right," Kevin agreed. "Man, we should hang out sometime. Any friend of Cam's…"

Matty knew exactly why that idea sent a thrill of excitement down his body, straight to his cock.

But no, this wasn't a hookup in a dark bar near Church and Wellesley. Kevin was a new guy in town and probably a little lonely, especially moving here from his hometown. This was gonna be his first time playing away from home. He needed buddies.

Just buddies, Matty told himself firmly. *You can do buddies.* He prayed Kevin wasn't angling for a wingman at the bars.

"Yeah!" Matty answered and clinked bottles again. "A friend of Cam's is a friend of mine, too. Go for drinks sometime?"

"That'd be great," Kevin agreed, and the grin on his face made Matty smile.

If nothing else, having a young, green player around who was just starting to see the world open up for him would be a change. With his own transition to the major leagues this fall, Matty felt exactly the same, only one step up.

Maybe they had even more in common than Cam.

Three

KEVIN

"ARE YOU GOING HIKING AGAIN THIS WEEK? MAYBE I SHOULD come." Kevin closed the cupboard doors, handing curry powder over to his roommate, Hans.

Hans was tall, a dual German-Canadian citizen, and kept to himself pretty well. He didn't have the money to pay for a trainer like Glenn. He'd told Kevin his plan was to work out on his own. He was biking, hiking, and swimming this summer. Frankly, that sounded more fun than gym work, even if it was less targeted and scientific.

"Oh, perhaps," Hans answered. He spoke English perfectly, but rapid-fire like he couldn't remember where one word or even sentence ended and the next began. "I don't know. I have to talk to a few of my buddies about it. I'll let you know. Curry's done, set the table."

"Yeah, cool," Kevin nodded and pushed away from the counter to grab forks and set the table. So far, they'd only been living together for a month but they got along pretty well. They had similar taste in food and neither of them were weekly partiers.

Hans had been on Kevin's team for two years now. "Hey, so, most of the guys I'm running into have been with the team — or the big boys' team — for a couple years now. Not a lot of newbies."

As Hans carried bowls of curry and rice to the table, he nodded. "Everyone's a second- or third-year, since the big reorganization."

"Right," Kevin nodded.

Hans was on the active reserve list right now, but that could change at prospect camp. For now, he'd taken Hans's spot on the team since they played the exact same position.

Kevin was glad Hans didn't seem too fussed, though. As a newbie, he'd likely be swapped in and out throughout the first season anyway. With more experience than him, Hans had a good shot of doing better.

"I'm happy where I am," Hans shrugged. "It might be a little less active this year, but I was a wreck after last season. If I don't have to stress about getting to top shape by September, my summer will be a lot happier."

Kevin couldn't understand that. If *he* was rotated out of the team this season, he planned to work his ass off to get back on it as soon as possible and earn his minutes on the ice so he could prove himself there.

The insatiable urge to keep getting better was almost a problem for Kevin. His goals were to build up his strength and stamina and ruthlessly massage out flaws in his technique and strategy.

"You could come swimming with me, though," Hans suggested. "I'm going after lunch."

Kevin groaned. "After curry?"

"It's not that bad! Don't overeat."

Although he complained and grumbled to make Hans

laugh, Kevin left a little room as he dumped out his bowl and washed up the dishes.

While Kevin trained at Glenn's gym daily, he also had a membership at the neighborhood gym. A lot of players living in this area did. It was solid, quiet, clean, had great equipment, and there was camaraderie with fellow players as well as civilians since it wasn't a pro-exclusive gym.

Best of all, they had a sauna, hot tub, and a swimming pool. Sometimes, after he woke up aching from a workout, Kevin went to the gym early just to sit in the hot tub until the janitor gave him concerned looks.

Today, though, he'd push himself into timing a few laps. He didn't rigorously time it, but the overall strength and muscles built by swimming beat many other types of cross-training. Best of all, there wasn't the same joint strain that came with pounding the pavement or a treadmill.

And it was fun to horse around in the pool sometimes. When Hans hesitated to climb into the pool, dunking his foot in first as he always did, Kevin grabbed it and hauled him down into the water.

Hans choked and coughed when he surfaced, then splashed him while Kevin laughed and dodged, splashing back with an open hand. He might not have brothers of his own, but he knew how to win a water fight.

"You ass!" Hans exclaimed, grabbing Kevin's arm to try to push him down into the water.

Kevin just laughed harder, inhaling the chlorine-scented air with the delight of a preteen boy. God, he hadn't had this much fun in a pool for years. On school trips to the local pool, where horsing around got disapproval from the teacher in the form of a—

"Hmph."

The distinctly disapproving noise was followed by the gentle splash of someone slipping into the pool.

Kevin cast a careless glance over his shoulder at whatever old bird had it in for fun.

Oh, shit.

It was Matty, and he was ducking under the divider to the closest lane. As he surfaced, despite Kevin's best efforts to glance away again, his eyes seemed to be glued to the older pro.

Water rivulets ran down Matty's back, between his angular shoulder blades and the straight, long line of his spine, dripping from the tips of his slicked-back hair. It was a scene straight from some cheesy movie — or soft-core porn, he tried desperately not to think — but that didn't detract from his interest.

"Hey, man," Kevin called out, trying to ignore the sudden dryness in his throat. He heard Hans chime in, but didn't really register his roommate's voice. He was more focused on getting a response — any response.

Fuck. He admired Matty — had watched him in all the games Cam had shown him, and more on his own. This was strictly professional. The pool tile was slick under his hand as he gripped the side of the pool, treading water.

Matty pulled himself back against the wall like a sprinter at the starting line and waved. Water droplets caught on his stubble and chest hair, and the edge of the water played over Matty's perky nipples.

And then Kevin was underwater, his asshole roommate shoving him under while he was distracted. Kevin kicked Hans's leg to make him let go of him as he surfaced, then splashed him once more full-on in the face for good measure. "C'mon, we gotta work out, not just play all day."

The sudden burst of focus was *not* brought on by glancing back again to see and hear those clean strokes cutting through the water.

This was another chance to impress people who mattered. Not that Matty was captain or had any say in the hiring decisions, but he didn't want to come off as unprofessional before he even started the team.

Despite Hans grumbling, Kevin pushed away from the wall and ducked under the divider once Matty was on the other side of the pool, then into the next lane. Hans had to take the other lane.

For a moment, Kevin's gaze was caught by those muscled arms rising from the water in swift, quick movements as Matty powered himself back towards their side. But fuck, *no*, Hans was right next to him. No way was he getting a hard-on in the pool. Not from and in front of some guy he wanted to impress.

He had to distract himself.

Kevin pushed himself against the wall, barely waiting to get into a good form before pushing himself off and through the water. Swimming with a semi wasn't the most comfortable, but it was a fuckload better than letting it get any further.

He quickly distracted himself from the sheer rhythm of keeping track of his strokes. Not the kind he wanted right now, but...

Fuck off, he told his intrusive thoughts.

Stroke, stroke, breathe.

Stroke, stroke—

"Fuck," he yelped when his hand cracked the side of the pool.

Look ahead, too, idiot, he told himself. Before he even

finished the thought, he cast an unconscious glance to the side to see if Matty had witnessed it.

Matty was clinging onto the wall there, his expression tightening for a moment. "All right?"

"Yeah," Kevin breathed out a quick laugh and shook it out.

Matty gave him a quick jerk of his chin, then pushed away again, streaking through the water.

Kevin waited a second or two to make it clear that he was *not* racing him, then pushed away a little less smoothly for a lap.

This time, he squinted ahead of him, through the water despite his blurry eyes, to keep an eye on the rapidly approaching pool wall. He hesitated with his last stroke or two, then grabbed the wall.

Now he had a sense for the length of the pool again, he could try a few other strokes. But front crawl was the best for practicing breath control.

"I hate the chlorine taste," Hans complained as he pushed off for his first slow lap. He clearly wasn't aiming for speed.

Matty smirked, his gaze flickering to Kevin after Hans was off. "That's probably not chlorine."

Kevin coughed on the chemical-laden air, then snorted with laughter and pushed himself into another couple laps.

The silence was more companionable now that Kevin knew Matty wasn't pissed at him and Hans for horsing around in the pool. They were probably a dozen laps in before Matty spoke up again. "You're not bad."

In fact, Kevin could probably keep up with Matty. He tried to remind himself that Matty had had a longer season than him, and that he was sleeker and had less drag to deal with, but his chest still swelled pridefully. "You, too."

They were both pulled up against the pool wall, and

Kevin saw the flash of competitiveness in Matty's eyes before he even said a word.

Kevin played dirty: he pushed away from the wall that second and cast Matty the quickest flash of a grin before surging forward. Matty was already in motion beside him, the force of the current from his strokes pushing lightly at Kevin as Kevin tried to break the water in front of them before Matty could.

If he'd thought Matty was swimming hard before, it was clear he'd been holding himself back.

Two could play that game. Kevin's back and shoulders stretched as he reached further, pulled himself harder, and kicked his legs harder than ever.

Then, in a shockingly small number of strokes, they were done.

No, they weren't. Matty was flipping underwater, just like on TV.

Kevin snorted, grabbing the wall and pulling it towards himself. He was on his back, but he didn't have time to correct that. He'd win unfairly if he had to.

On his back, he felt even stronger. He watched the ceiling tiles above him to keep straight in his lane as he closed the gap between him and Matty. Or so he hoped. He couldn't really look over and see this way, but he felt rippling water lapping against his side, so he was close.

Then the back of his hand was smacking the wall, and as he looked over, Matty's hand was closing around the wall.

Too fucking close to call.

The burn in Kevin's muscles and lungs reminded him of sweaty nights under the sheets with someone. His ex-partner, maybe, or a random guy. He hadn't dated since moving here. He needed to change that soon.

Matty grinned at him, his dark eyes sparkling. "Again?"

"Again," Kevin told him, even though he was heaving for breath, he pushed himself into motion. Kevin watched as Matty flipped over to his back, waiting until he pushed away before he straightened out his legs to push himself away again.

This time, Kevin hit the wall a good half-second before Matty, but he didn't waste a second turning to race back to the start.

And he won that one by a second.

"Nice." Matty gave him an easygoing smile, but Kevin could see it in his eyes: he hated to lose. He knew that feeling all too well.

That led to another two laps, then another.

Now, Matty was winning. He had better stamina, and it was starting to piss Kevin off. He wasn't a dick, though. He nodded his acknowledgement every time Matty beat him.

"Jesus, you two burn out all your energy now," Hans snorted. "Go ahead."

Kevin jolted. Shit, he'd almost forgotten he was there.

"No, I'm done." Matty pushed himself out of the pool easily, his biceps and triceps bulging as he hopped up onto the edge of the pool. His swim trunks clung for a moment to his bulge, right at eye level...

Kevin hauled his eyes over to Hans instead, his nails digging into the tiles. "I think I wore myself out, too." He waited until Matty strode into the locker room entrance before raising an eyebrow at Hans to ask what that sudden exit was about.

"He gets in a zone," Hans told him, his voice low to avoid having it carry over the water of the pool. "Don't mind it."

Kevin glanced at the entrance to the locker rooms. He

had an idea of the knot that might be tying up Matty's chest, because there was one in his own chest despite the fun competition.

Did Matty fear losing, even something this insignificant? Nah, maybe that was Kevin projecting his own issues onto Matty.

JESUS. WHY HADN'T HE BEEN ABLE TO KEEP HIS RAZOR-SHARP focus with Kevin around? He was used to swimming with hot guys — hot teammates, even — around. Hell, even buff dudes, stripping in the locker room right in front of him didn't do much for him anymore.

It wasn't just proximity.

Yeah, Kevin *was* exactly his type — sleek but muscled, with a six-pack he would love to run his tongue over and full lips that would look perfect dragging down the length of his cock.

But it wasn't just looks, either. It was that fire in Kevin's eye when he'd flicked his eyes towards the other wall, responding to Matty's unspoken challenge without a second thought.

And Kevin had won the first couple laps, stinging Matty's pride.

Well, he'd cheated the first one, but Matty had been slow, distracted by the flash of a mischievous grin splitting that gorgeous face.

But Matty had so fucking much to focus on. Like, shit, not getting bumped back down. He'd only gotten called up at the end of last season. They hadn't called him up *for* the play-offs, meaning he wasn't their first pick. They were counting on him getting into shape before the season began. Then, he'd get a few sheltered minutes here and there, carefully testing his abilities.

He'd really only gotten called up because Cam — by all accounts a better player, with more points and fewer flaws — had collapsed on ice, and he'd been their number two choice. Maybe even number three or four.

Matty couldn't throw away this chance.

Voices echoed down the hall and Matty quickly yanked the shower knob to turn the shower water off, then grabbed his towel to run once over his hair, face, and torso before wrapping it around his waist.

Not that he didn't think he had self-control around the guy, but just in case. Adrenaline did funny things sometimes.

"Hey," Kevin greeted, that warm voice sending a shiver of pleasure straight through Matty. A nice, sexy, rough voice did *everything* for and to him, but nobody had to know that.

"Hey," Matty answered briefly, walking over to the lockers while his toes curled into the damp, lemon-scented floor. He stepped around the yellow *floor wet, caution* sign and pulled open his locker. "Nice work back there."

"You too." Kevin sounded sincere. "You're good. You swam as a kid?"

"Yeah." Matty laughed under his breath. "About all there is to do in my damn town."

"I know the feeling," Kevin laughed, and Matty smiled despite himself. "I bet Cam bitched about Fredericton a few times."

Matty hesitated, but didn't comment on the word choice. He just coolly answered, "Yeah." He pulled his change of clothes out of the locker.

Kevin slammed his locker shut and headed for the shower, and Matty didn't glance after him. Hans followed a minute later.

Matty let out a breath, stepping out of his towel and into trunks, then jeans. He buttoned them up and toweled his torso off so he could force his t-shirt onto his damp torso.

He still smelled like the pool, but that was fine. He wasn't trying to impress anyone.

By the time he was sitting down to slip his sandals on again, Kevin was on the other side of the locker room stepping into his clothes.

"So, how long have you been living here, then?" Matty asked, to make a bit of conversation.

"A month," Kevin told him. When Matty glanced back, he was at least wearing jeans. Thank God.

"Liking it?"

"Like I said: there's a lot I miss about Fredericton, but none of those things are Fredericton."

Matty laughed at that way of putting it. Sounded a lot like Timmins, his hometown. "Going home soon?"

"For a bit. I think I'll take a week."

"Only?" Most of the guys spent at least a couple weeks, maybe a month or more, at home recuperating and catching up. Then again, Kevin had only just moved out.

"Yeah. You?"

Matty hummed and shrugged. "I can't say anything. I'm thinking about just a week, too."

"You live round here?"

"Yep," Matty told him. "Liberty Village."

Kevin whistled. "Right around the corner from me! Well, and a few blocks. But I can't get over how many of us are around here."

"It's a nice neighborhood," Matty nodded. "If you wanna see more of it sometime…" he trailed off. Shit, was he offering to give guided tours to the guy? Who the fuck had let his dick in charge of things?

He was *not* watching Kevin shirtless.

Matty shouldered his gym bag — the lighter one he used for just the things he didn't keep locked up here.

But Kevin was already beaming, that brilliant smile cracking his face in two again. His teeth gleamed with the smile. "Thanks, man. Yeah, we should hang out."

"Tell each other stories about Cam," Matty offered with a laugh. He tried to ignore the awkward shift from Hans. Hans had never really been close to Cam, which made the conversation a bit awkward. They didn't have anything against each other, but groups were bound to form in any group of a couple dozen or more players. First line and fourth line forwards — active reserve forwards now — didn't automatically hang out.

Neither did pro and minor league players, but he was resolutely ignoring that. Kevin needed a buddy to help introduce him to his new teammates, and Matty could do that. He liked hanging around guys with his own level of determination, and it was already obvious from his pre-season and college-level play that Kevin had that in spades.

Hans, though…

Speaking of awkward.

"Anyway, I gotta go." Fisher and Chris would already be waiting for him at the shawarma place by the time he dropped his shit off at home. "Catch you later, man. See you, Hans."

Hans just grunted and raised a hand despite his extra effort, but Kevin gave him another quick, brilliant smile when he poked his head through his t-shirt and it fell into place over those beautiful abs.

Out of here, now. Matty grabbed for the locker room door and pulled it open before he could invent some other stupid excuse to talk to the guy.

***

"What kept you so long?"

"Got carried away swimming, missed the tram by a minute… you know how it goes," Matty sighed as he flopped down onto the comfortable stool with his shawarma in its waxy wrapping. This wasn't a fancy place, so he didn't feel bad keeping his buddies waiting to order from some leather-bound menu.

He picked up the laminated sheet and turned it over, even though he already knew what he wanted to order.

Now he was going to give the damn guy tours? Hang out and drink with him? He still couldn't believe he'd offered that. But what made him different from any other new guy he'd welcome to the team? Well, he wasn't on his team anymore.

Literally, that was. Who knew about the metaphorical team?

"So that new guy, Kevin," Fisher said, jolting Matty straight back to the moment. For a brief, irrational moment, he feared he'd said all that out loud.

"Yeah?"

"The one you met the other night—"

"I know," Matty rolled his eyes. "We talked about Fredericton and shit. He knows Cam."

"Right!" Chris grinned. "And Cam wound up being gay, right?"

Matty folded his arms and leaned back. "You're not gonna do the *all gay men know each other* thing, are you?"

"No!" Fisher laughed. "But, you know, he never goes out to bars, right? And he never picks up."

Matty tried not to feel so defensive. It wasn't like he really knew the guy yet. "So? Neither do I."

Chris leaned in with a deadpan expression, his eyes sparkling. "You have something you wanna tell us, man?"

Matty wasn't sure he liked that his instinctive reaction was to laugh it off. Fuck, these guys were his closest buddies out here, probably even including his friends back home. If he were gonna tell anybody, it would have to be them.

But things were different. He was in the top league now. You didn't just come out before your first season there even started.

And Fisher and Chris weren't smiling now, both watching him as if expecting to hear a serious answer.

Holy shit, was he that obvious?

Matty held it a second longer, then laughed loudly. "Gotcha."

"You fucker," Chris exclaimed while Fisher broke the tension with a laugh, then punched his arm. "I thought you were serious there."

"Course not." Matty waved the menu at Fisher and Chris until it made a *wub-wub* plastic rattling sound, then tossed it to the table. "You ready to order?"

The three hockey players piled after one another, still

shoving each other and laughing about how *of course* he didn't have anything to tell them.

It was only when they were back at the table, Matty cradling his wrapped-up shawarma, that Chris returned to the subject. "But if he is, I wouldn't blame him for not coming out yet. We'd be cool with it, but… you never know. That's a big weak spot to show."

Don't flinch, Matty told himself. It *was* a weak spot as far as the game went. Matty knew they meant his wellbeing on ice, not that it was wrong in general. "Huh? He's probably just focused on work like me. Don't read too much into it. God."

Fisher looked sympathetic. "Man, you're still freaking out? You don't need that shit."

"Preseason hasn't even started. Pre-*pre*-training season hasn't started!" Chris snorted and kicked his chair. "Dude, relax. You've got talent, that's why they called you up. Don't worry so much."

The compliments felt hollow to Matty, and he smiled and waved them off. It was true—he had a two-week break before training season and camps properly started. He was gonna ask Glenn what he could do over the break to keep in shape. Maybe only visit home for half the time, then come back here to work out…

He tried to focus on their discussions of baseball, but his heart wasn't in it. At least the shawarma was fantastic as always, and he didn't have to worry about his meal plan yet, either.

That would come soon enough.

CHAPTER
Five

KEVIN

THE ROPE BURNED AGAINST HIS PALMS, BUT KEVIN convulsively clenched his fists tighter and gritted his teeth through the pain.

His muscles were exhausted, oxygen-starved, and he needed to breathe deeper and haul himself up harder.

The gym wall had never seemed so high.

"C'mon," he hissed to himself. *I know I can do better than this.*

He was two arms-lengths from the top of the rope.

One…

Do it. Come on. His own body weight felt insurmountable, and his knees ached from scrambling and bumping against the gym wall as if it would give him more traction. But this was it: the end of his hardest drill today.

Two!

Kevin grabbed the top of the rope and gasped for breath, but he didn't want to hold himself up for long. He was supposed to come down as slowly as he could stand, though.

"Hey, Glenn. How's it going?"

Kevin nearly froze on the rope. From somewhere below, that was Matty's unmistakable friendly bellow.

"Hey, not bad for an old fellow. What's got into you? You look like you're ready to run a mile."

"Post-season fatigue's wearing off, I guess," Matty answered. Kevin twisted to get a better look as he paused halfway down the wall, but he could just make out a hint of a friendly grin from this angle.

"Just in time for your break."

"Actually, that's what I wanted a word about," Matty told Glenn. "I'm not going home the whole time, just the first week. Then I'm coming back here for another week of prep before the first camp."

"Uh huh," Glenn answered. "You're sure you're up for that?"

"Positive," Matty answered as Kevin touched the floor. He didn't look over his way yet, he was so focused on their trainer instead. He looked like he was seeking permission like a man in a desert might cajole the keeper of the spring.

Kevin knew that even thinking up that metaphor meant he needed to drink more water. He grabbed his water bottle to chug down another half a liter, trying to subtly lurk nearby to listen in.

"Okay," Glenn finally nodded. "I can't stop you, and you *are* in good shape relative to the rest of the guys."

"Yes," Matty pumped his fist.

"I'll give you a list of suggested exercises for that week."

Matty had caught sight of him, and he raised his hand in a wave.

Kevin licked his lips and waved back, then approached the other two. "Hey. I heard you're staying here for a week? So am I."

"No kidding," Matty smiled. "Cool. Yeah, I was just asking Glenn about stuff I can do on my own."

"You two should hook up."

Kevin didn't expect that to make his cheeks heat up. Thank God he was already red and sweating from hauling himself up that damn rope. *Get your mind out of the gutter!*

"You're both moving up a level this year, so you both have some pretty strong incentive to work out, huh?" Glenn asked, glancing between them. "And you've got similar work ethics."

Matty was already nodding, so Kevin did, too.

"I'd like that," Matty agreed. "We'll try to sync up schedules. You signed up there or were you just on a pool pass the other day?"

"Patson's? Yeah, I'm signed up there."

"Good," Matty told him. "All the local boys are."

Glenn nodded. "That's set, then. Go on, both of you, get out to the yard and stretch it out." He kicked a medicine ball nearby. "Grab one each."

They each grabbed a medicine ball and headed out to the yard as instructed. Kevin took deep breaths of the early summer air, unable to help smiling. God, it was nice not to be buried under snow and bleak grey skies.

"You just finishing your workout?" Matty asked.

Kevin sighed as he flopped over a medicine ball and rolled slowly down it, stretching out his back a bit at a time. "Yeah. Just getting here?"

"Yep." Matty chuckled. "We'll try to sync up our workouts."

"Sounds great." Kevin grunted when he reached that spot in his lower back. "Man, beginning of summer, you always feel like such a… flabby duck."

Matty laughed loudly. "The fuck? That's a weird…"

"Sorry," Kevin snorted. "I'm the king of weird analogies when I'm tired. My brain just tries to go to the nearest possible words…"

Matty chuckled. "Yeah, I've had a couple buddies who talk like that when they're drunk. Not a lot else to do in northern Ontario."

Sounded familiar. Kevin grimaced. "Yeah, I bet. That's where you're from?"

"Yep. Not a lot there except… mines, and a couple stores… schools, more or less… Jesus, I'm glad to be out of there."

Kevin winced. "Fredericton isn't that bad. It's only a day's drive away from New York or Montreal, if you really need a break."

Matty nodded, pulling himself off the ball. He flopped back-first onto it and carefully stretched out his back again. "I'm always glad to be home for the first week and I hate being there the second week."

"So you're dealing with that problem before it even starts." Kevin did a few crunches while he was at it, his hands laced behind his head. His core was still recovering from yesterday's workout, so he'd gone a little too easy on himself today.

"Bingo," Matty laughed. "What about you?"

"I've never played higher than university level," Kevin admitted. "Big learning curve."

"Getting ahead of the jump. Smart, too."

"We can keep stroking each other's egos all day," Kevin smirked, then cast a quick sideways glance at Matty. A lot of guys messed around with fake-gay comments, but it was sometimes hard to read new friends until it was too late.

Matty laughed, though, and Kevin relaxed. "You looking forward to getting home, though? You gotta say hi to Cam for me."

"Oh, I will," Kevin promised. "A buddy of mine's been going through a rough patch, actually. Sounds like things are up with his parents."

Matty winced. "Yeah? He our age or younger?"

"A bit older, actually," Kevin sighed. "But living in the same town as your parents..."

"Yeah," Matty drawled. "That's hard, I imagine."

Kevin couldn't talk about his buddies behind their backs, so he left it there. "And I get to see my family before the season begins."

"Yeah, good idea," Matty told him. "It's gonna be a long year, your first one. I'm just gonna go out with my buds, and maybe out hiking with my dog."

"Aw, you got a dog?" Kevin grinned. It didn't surprise him at all. Matty seemed like a dog guy. "Cute."

"Shut up," Matty laughed, peeling himself off the medicine ball once he'd stretched his arms out. "Catch."

Kevin hauled himself upright just in time to catch the huge, mercifully lightweight medicine ball before it bounced off his face. "Hey!" He tossed it back and laughed, then caught it again as they tossed it back and forth, helping Matty limber up and him cool off.

It was nice just to hang out and chat with this guy, if he could only stop noticing in inconvenient moments how fucking hot he was.

"Okay, Glenn's gonna come drag me in by the hair if I procrastinate any more. But I'm switching my slot to later so we can be off the same time tomorrow, so he can show us what to do next week."

"Great." Kevin was thrilled at the thought of working out with Matty, even if it was intimidating. "Good luck, man. I gotta get home. Let's go for drinks after the gym tomorrow, yeah?"

"Yeah!" Matty agreed, and Kevin was taken aback by that enthusiastic grin. He had a brilliant white smile—the kind of grin that made him instinctively want to grin back.

Kevin realized he was staring and jerked his head in a quick nod, then grabbed his medicine ball to bring back inside. "Cool. See you tomorrow, bro."

Kinda sad. That's the closest to a date I've gotten in months.

CHAPTER
Six

MATTY

"You're it!"

"Oh, you motherf—get back here!"

Matty stumbled to a halt as he pushed the side gate of the gym open only to find four guys in the middle of what looked like a game of tag.

Then, Klein was slapping his shoulder as he sprinted past Matty. "It! Move or play!"

"Reciprocal tags allowed?" Matty yelled as he dropped his gym bag and took off after him.

Kevin was nearby and laughing, jogging backwards to stay well clear of Matty's path. "Nope!"

Matty turned on his heel and closed the gap between him and Kevin in a few easy strides, dodging around the field goalposts when Kevin tried to use them as shelter.

God, he could just take Kevin down…

Matty slapped Kevin's shoulder. "It," he winked.

Kevin stumbled and glared, but he was breathlessly laughing, too. He was so cute when his cheeks were pink.

No, shit, he had to stop thinking that before he hung out with the guy regularly.

Unless, of course, Kevin's little fidget when Glenn told them to hook up had meant *that*.

Matty stayed out of the way as Kevin took off to tag Klein right back. He had a big advantage over the rest of them: one of his main skills was sprinting. Every coach had told him he was light and quick on his feet, which helped with his aggressive point-scoring style.

That made games like this almost no fun, because he could evade the others for long enough for them to get bored and choose another target. The only exception was Kevin: he could keep ahead of him, but only barely. Being challenged was both hot and irritating.

When Glenn came to yell that the game was over and tell them to get their asses inside, Matty jogged back to the gate to grab his bag. Kevin was nearby, leaning on the fence for a moment to catch his breath.

"You're quick," Matty told him.

Kevin winked, then rubbed his arm down his face and shook his head. "You too. I can't believe I couldn't get you there."

Matty laughed. "It was close, though, man." He clapped Kevin's arm as they set off towards the gym side door together. "Just got here?"

"Yep, this was our warmup." Kevin's eyes sparkled with a moment of childlike joy. "Been years since I played tag."

"What a warmup, huh?" Matty grinned. "Now you know why the guys like him. It's not just grunt work. He finds ways of making it fun."

Kevin nodded. "I don't care how fun it is, as long as the end results are worth it, but... I'm weird."

Matty totally understood what he meant. Some guys got bored—in other words, lazy—when their exercise programs were too same-samey. He didn't care—he'd eat the same meal ten days in a row, or do the same workout ten days in a row, if it was effective. He high-fived Kevin and jerked his chin in a quick nod. "Agreed."

"Cool," Kevin grinned, then held the door for Matty to head through.

Once Matty dropped off his gear, he went to find Glenn, but the smirk on his face made Matty slow his steps. "Oh, no."

Glenn laughed. "It's not a *bad* thing. I just noticed you're in pretty good shape considering where we are in your recovery period." Kevin was standing next to him and laughing under his breath.

"Which means I get to do what?"

"You're both doing sleds."

Oh, boy. Pulling weighted sleds across the field was usually a little later in the season, or even in their intensive week-long training camp. Glenn must have thought they were in fine form.

Matty wasn't convinced, but if Glenn thought he could handle it, he'd do it.

"Go get ready."

Matty stripped his t-shirt off and dumped it on a bench by the door, then grabbed his water bottle and headed to the weights area.

Glenn was already there, handing them the ropes of two weighted sleds. "Out you two get."

Kevin's sled looked about heavy as his: a hundred pounds. Not a lot, especially for guys like them, but the idea was a low weight and more reps.

"You know the drill, Matty. You wanna talk Kevin through the unloaded ones, and I'll get these guys set up?"

Matty nodded, leading Kevin to the turf outside. "Right. We do a couple unloaded reps just to get used to having the harness on, then a set of twenty loaded reps, improving our form with everything Glenn tells us. Then a couple more reps without the harness on, and you'll be blazing. We do a lot of this during the camp. He must want you to be familiar with it."

Kevin was studying him and nodding, taking note of every word he said. Those cute pink lips pinched together with focus, making it really hard to focus on anything but them.

It was pretty easy to get the harness on and the sled unloaded, and then Matty went first to demonstrate. Just before he took off, Glenn stepped outside to supervise them both until they started the weighted reps.

Matty focused totally on his body, keeping himself leaning forward and his feet positioned just as he'd been taught. His main focus was on his form, and he kept an ear out for any corrections from Glenn.

Once it was Kevin's turn, the guy took easily to corrections and seemed focused on his own performance. Matty could already see what Glenn meant about his work ethic; Kevin seemed to want to work out as hard as he could. No wonder, given what they were paying for training.

Then they were left alone for the remainder of their reps, watching each other's forms.

Kevin was really giving her, as his American teammates would tease him for saying. Matty could watch Kevin shirtless, the harness straining against his hips, all day long. Sweat trickled down along his chest and over his smooth stomach, and ran down the hollowed ridge of his spine. His hair clung to his forehead, his lips parted for deep breaths, his eyes bright and absolutely focused.

He looked like he'd be deadly on ice.

Once they were done, the harnesses off, practicing sprinting together down the field, it felt like Matty was flying. He barely felt the ground under him without the weight behind him.

And Kevin was there by his side, breath rasping at his lungs, the occasional grunts as his feet hit the ground and propelled himself forward.

For some reason, it was an emotional moment.

Then they slowed as they reached the fence at the other end of the field, and Kevin whooped and grabbed him around the shoulders to haul him in for back-slapping cele-bration.

"That was fast as *lightning*," Matty grinned, clapping Kevin right back and bumping their chests together.

Their bare, hot, sweaty chests rubbed together, and fuck, for a second, Matty couldn't get the image out of his head: Kevin's body under his as they moved together, fast and hard, in the sheets.

Matty pulled back abruptly with another punch to Kevin's shoulder, then strode down the field towards the gym again while Kevin jogged to catch up with him. "Fuckin' great," he told Kevin.

"Yeah," Kevin panted. "Awesome. That *did* feel like... flying. Wow. I've never felt like that, except on ice. And maybe skis."

Matty laughed. "You ski?"

"I have. Cross-training. Not much, though. Ski season is skating season, so..."

"Nothing happens during skating season," Matty nodded. "Man, you've got better abs than me." He reached to playfully try to slap them while Kevin twisted away and laughed. "The fuck did you do that for?"

"I can show you my crunches," Kevin offered with a grin. "I add an extra twist."

Matty jerked his head in a nod and elbowed Kevin's arm, pushing him off-course before taking off in a jog for the building. It was great to find a buddy who didn't mind joshing around, too. "That'd be sweet."

Kevin kept his voice down as they approached the building. "It's so great to do things other than, like, pilates and monkey bars."

Matty laughed. "I know, it seems boring, but trust him. All the tumbling and handstands and toning shit helps when you come out of a rough season next year."

"Yeah," Kevin nodded. "Especially if we go all the way."

It took an embarrassing second longer than it should have for Matty to finish, *To the playoffs.* "Right," he quickly nodded. "All right, let's see what other hell he wants to put us through." Despite his complaint, he was grinning, and so was Kevin.

There was nothing like the adrenaline that surged through his body when he was working out, except the thrill of an actual game.

Or...

No, he had to keep his mind off Kevin's cute little ass.

The first thing Matty noticed when they stripped in the locker room after their workout was, of course, Kevin. His ass wasn't so little, actually. Hockey players had the best asses. It was a shame Matty hadn't managed to find a hockey guy to date, really.

Matty pushed the thought aside. Locker rooms had stopped being scary—dangerous, even—after his first few years. Now, he could see dicks and asses all day long and not react at all, even to hot, flirtatious, smart, fit guys slapping him on the ass.

But Kevin? One look at Kevin and he wanted to crowd up into his space and kiss him?

This was something completely new for him.

"So we're going downtown to get a bite to eat and a drink?" Kevin asked, snapping Matty from his reverie of staring at the shower water tap while scrubbing his body off.

"Yeah, sure," Matty agreed. "Anything you feel like?"

"I know a pulled pork place, about ten or fifteen minutes away."

That sounded like heaven, actually. Matty grinned and turned off the water, then headed for the benches. "Sold to the man in… nothing at all."

Kevin's sharp, surprised laugh echoed off all four tiled walls of the shower room.

They dressed in relative comfortable silence, politely ignoring the groan or two they heard from each other when they bent this way or that to get dressed.

"Long day here, wasn't it?" Matty finally asked as they locked away their gym bags.

Kevin nodded hard. "God, yeah. I like it, though."

"It's the best job ever."

"It is."

They waved their goodbyes to Glenn on the way out,

then set off down the sidewalk. The spring air felt even more pleasant drying Matty's damp hair from the shower.

Matty's worry about what he'd say when he was alone—as much as possible on the sidewalk of Toronto—with the guy vanished after Kevin brought up last week's trades. Before they knew it, they were at the pulled pork sandwich place, passionately discussing Carter jumping to the west coast.

"I played with him, though," Matty repeated himself. "I know the guy."

Kevin conceded the point and huffed, raising his hands and letting Matty open the door for him. "Fine, but I still think it's gonna be a mistake."

"Is it a loyalty thing?" Matty asked, raising a brow. God, this place smelled divine. As he followed Kevin in, he inhaled deeply.

Kevin hesitated, then grimaced. "Yeah, probably. It just leaves a bad taste in my mouth, doing all that work with Coach Walker and then jumping ship the second some team with a better record offers. If guys didn't do that, you wouldn't see the skewed stats you do. Instead you have teams who've never won, even though there's plenty of great guys that have played with them."

Matty chuckled quietly. "It's always gonna happen, man. Whatcha having?"

"The original. That's the best. Their gravies are good, though," Kevin told him.

Matty wound up ordering the same as Kevin, and when they sat down to devour their double-meat sandwiches and kill the workout hunger beast within, he was glad he'd chosen that. It *was* a damn good sandwich.

"Wanna go to the museum, kill some time before the pub? I feel like a loser if I drink before five," Kevin grinned.

"Yeah, sure," Matty laughed. He had a keen sense of humor and strong opinions in addition to that pretty face, clever mind, and good style on the ice. He was in danger of crushing on the guy if he wasn't careful.

And Kevin was watching him a lot, smiling readily, laughing at even his bad jokes. He was the kind of guy it was nice to kill time with. Matty just hoped they were on the same page here.

KEVIN

"I ALWAYS THOUGHT THEY WERE MAGIC, MAN."

Kevin cast Matty a surprised glance. Through the whole geology exhibit, he'd been passionate about all these rocks, and Kevin couldn't quite get it. He could see Matty being a rock nerd as a kid, but there was more there, too.

"Geodes? Crystals hidden inside ordinary rocks, bro. Of course they're magic," Kevin grinned, moving past the enormous grey rock that had been cracked open to reveal the jagged purple spikes of crystal within. "You really like these rocks."

"Yeah," Matty half-smiled, turning to look around at the exhibits along the walls of the museum. "Don't you?"

"I just hate the way they're presented."

Matty looked confused for a moment.

"With all the mining propaganda." Kevin rubbed a hand over his hair, then went to touch the rock wall, tracing the vein through it. "I guess that's a strong word, but…"

Matty was watching him.

"All the mine closures out east, you know," Kevin finished

with a shrug. "Left a lot of my buddies in trouble, especially what with Alberta these days."

"But that's not your fault. It's the provincial government. They haven't been supporting any of the mining towns properly," Matty said, and Kevin couldn't tear his eyes away from the passion in his expression. "Mines might not last forever, but mining *can* be a smart short-term strategy to set up something sustainable. I mean, if damn Queen's Park stops holding onto the money they owe us."

Kevin nodded slowly. "Yeah, we don't get a lot of it out our way either, man."

"Fuckin' Alberta."

Kevin laughed. "I think everyone but Albertans agrees on that. God, it's rough right now, though."

"Yeah, I feel a little sorry for them," Matty admitted, then glanced at Kevin. "But, bro, so many of the guys just blew their money out there! I don't feel bad for *them*."

Kevin snorted and nodded. Everyone knew guys going out for an easy six-figure job and wasting it all on booze. And housing, of course.

"A seventy grand salary like the old days—I guess like what you've got now?" Matty toasted Kevin with an imaginary bottle of beer and Kevin nodded. "That was a huge step up for me. But the first thing I did was start saving."

"Right." Kevin was kind of impressed, actually. So many players their age blew most of their money. Matty seemed way more grounded than your average guy.

He tried not to think about what an attractive trait that was in a lover. It was also interesting in a friend, of course.

"This gold is cool, though," Kevin spoke up to distract Matty from getting back to his political rant.

Matty smiled easily and ran his finger along the vein of

gold through the stones. "Yeah, it is. This place is pretty cool, though. Propaganda or no," he winked.

Kevin's cheeks felt hot. He glared at Matty and rolled his eyes. "You're the one who's all *fuck Queen's Park*," he snorted. "But yeah, Toronto does an okay job with its museums."

"And a lot of stuff. I mean, Toronto sucks, but I feel lucky to be here." After his sudden revelation, Matty walked towards the exhibit entrance.

Kevin strode to catch up. "Me, too. Ready for the pub yet?"

"Definitely. No more politics," Matty promised with a laugh and clapped Kevin's shoulder. His hand lingered on his upper back for a few moments too long, and Kevin resisted the urge to bump their shoulders.

Matty cast him a quick glance, scanning his expression before pulling his hand back.

That look… That wasn't a normal straight guy look, not even by Kevin's standards. He didn't comment on it, but it felt like they walked a little closer on their way to the pub.

"So if Toronto isn't it… what's your dream team?" Matty asked.

"Are we talking my level or yours?"

Matty laughed. "Either. Say mine, then."

"Oooh, boy," Kevin laughed. "Depends on the coach. By the time I get there, they could be totally different. But Vancouver or Florida, just for the weather."

"Yeah." Matty snorted. "Fuck Toronto winters, honestly."

Kevin grinned. "And Fredericton winters."

"And… pretty much all Canadian winters."

"We should just become cruise ship workers," Kevin elbowed Matty. "Entertainers."

"You play any instruments?"

"Not yet," Kevin laughed. "But I could learn the guitar. I was kinda halfway through learning as a teen."

"Oh, great idea," Matty ribbed him. "I'll be the halfway-good dancer, you be the halfway-good guitar player. We'll do a sketch."

"At least we'd be warm while we're being heckled," Kevin shrugged.

Matty smiled. "Seriously though, man… you know what happened to Cam?"

Who didn't? Cameron Riley, one of Kevin's good friends, had been one of the top picks for the draft until his sudden heart condition. It had taken months to even diagnose, and by that point, it was way too late to get back into the game.

Rather, Coach Walker would have taken Cam back, but Cam had decided he was done.

"Of course," Kevin nodded. "Rough, losing your job and your life like that all at once."

Cam hadn't suffered too much; he'd jumped into beekeeping, found a boyfriend, and moved into a commune-like situation with his brothers. Well, each of them had their own house, but to Kevin it was a little weird.

"You got a backup plan?" Matty asked, peering seriously between him and the sidewalk as they turned the corner and waited to cross.

Kevin shifted uncomfortably. "Not really. Seeing Cam… it did make me wonder if I should come up with a backup career. I'll tell you right fuckin' now, if I lose this job…"

Matty grimaced. "God forbid."

"Yeah," Kevin nodded. "But I'm spending a year picking up some kind of skill and running with it. I'm not gonna sit around and watch my greatest replays."

Matty pushed open the pub door and held it for Kevin. "Me, too. Hope it doesn't come to that, though."

Kevin nodded, his eyes wandering around the pub furnishings. This was a cute little place—a mural of British gentlemen on horses with a pack of dogs, wearing silly top hats added a certain levity.

They grabbed a couple beers and relaxed into the button-backed benches of the place, the dark wood table adding an extra coziness to the atmosphere. It could have easily felt too stuffy for him at night, but it seemed like the kind of place that was a lot more casual in the afternoon.

"I don't know, though," Kevin shook his head. "I've watched you play. I don't think you have anything to worry about."

Matty half-smiled. "Everyone always tells me that, man," he laughed. "But bro, I don't know."

"Same here, though," Kevin shook his head. "Especially since nobody here knows me."

"Coach Walker wouldn't have chosen you if he didn't see potential," Matty said, and the utter confidence in his voice bolstered Kevin with a glow of pride. "The team's all glad to have you around, man. Don't worry."

"And *you* shouldn't worry, either," Kevin held out his bottle for a toast and clinked them together, drinking deeply. "You earned your spot."

Matty looked a little flustered, quickly scanning the other tables instead of looking at Kevin. "Thanks."

He doesn't take praise well, then. Kevin just nodded, changing the subject to draft picks. It was something they could talk about without even thinking as they drank a couple beers and let the ache settle out of their muscles.

Kevin wasn't even sure how much time passed before he

realized it was getting into evening and he still had to pack for the week away, plus buy stuff for his buddies back home.

"And I gotta walk the dog."

"What's his name? Or her?"

"Jasmine." Matty rubbed his head. "That was her name when she came from the shelter."

"Jasmine's a pretty name," Kevin smiled. "And a shelter dog, too." Matty slid up a few notches in his estimation once again.

They set off through the park, strolling easily side by side. It was a friendly kind of camaraderie that kept them bantering, jostling each other's sides, sometimes bumping into each other and grinding shoulders for a pace or two before being shoved off with laughter.

As they reached Queen's Park, Kevin leaned in and whispered, "Now's your chance to make a difference."

"Huh?"

"You can start a rally."

Matty burst out laughing. "Oh, shut up. That was hours ago. You're the clever type, aren't you? Not gonna let anything go?" he winked.

"Definitely not." Kevin came to a halt in front of the statue, not paying it any mind. Matty's cheeks were flushed, his hair stuck up at odd angles. He stood with his weight shifted onto one leg, his hip stuck out and hand in his pocket.

Best of all, Matty's eyes were on Kevin's lips.

Neither of them said a word as they leaned in. It was fucking incredible, considering how much anxiety and worry and second-guessing he ought to have gone through first. Kevin *should* have been questioning it to the last second.

Instead, it was the most natural thing in the world to forgo the back-slapping bro hug.

Kevin's palms were cupping Matty's cheeks, while his hands landed on his back and hip. Matty wasn't pushing him away, and he even angled his head just a little.

Their lips met with a burst of warmth and pleasure, Kevin's chest and cock and even the tips of his fingers and toes all buzzing with excitement. Holy shit, *this* was what chemistry felt like. He'd half-forgotten, burying his urges under practices and homework of gameplay videos.

Just before Kevin tangled his hand in Matty's hair to keep him kissing him, he came to his senses.

Holy crap. Ohhhh, no, I didn't.

Kevin pulled back abruptly and raised a hand. He strode out of the park almost as fast as he could. It was all he could do to keep it to a fast walk and not a sprint.

Shit, shit, shit. I hope I didn't just fuck this up.

He hadn't just flung himself at the nearest guy to take him out for a drink and a day of sightseeing, had he?

Fuck, this was bad.

"Jasmine, don't lick Fleet's face. Bite his balls instead."

"Matty!" Fleet laughed from the backseat, but he kept petting Matty's dog anyway. "God, you asshole."

Matty grinned unrepentantly. "She's too nice, don't worry."

Fleet and his front-seat passenger, Derek, were second-years on his new pro team. When he'd heard they were both heading up to Sudbury, the halfway stop on his route home, Matty jumped at the chance to drive them both home.

It felt like a bit of infiltration, figuring out the team culture so he could join in as soon as their first events began.

"Prospects camp is coming up fast, eh?" Matty commented.

Derek nodded, turning to look back at Fleet so he could hear him. "Sure is. Everyone's just beat right now, sure. Hoping we all get back in shape in time."

"It'll whip us back into shape," Fleet laughed. "You were doing great at the gym the other day. Someone told me Glenn had you doing sleds."

Matty almost beamed. "Yeah, he did! I nearly pissed myself when he told me. I'm the only guy—me and Kevin, rather—he told to do that yet."

"You won't be able to next year," Fleet laughed. "Assuming we make the playoffs, of course. Like we will."

"Duh," Matty agreed easily, running a hand back through his hair. "I'm ready for it, I think."

Derek grinned. "Good. Man, it'll be a trip for your first year, though. You got any autograph-seekers yet?"

"One or two," Matty admitted. "They caught me at the store, weirdly enough. Not even at the gym or anything."

"It'll get weirder," Fleet promised him. "I mean, we're not even big names yet, and we're pretty popular. Especially with fangirls."

Derek laughed. "God, if I didn't have my girl back home."

"I keep telling you, long-distance won't work out."

Derek glared at Fleet. "It's going fine, thanks."

"Your loss," Fleet shrugged.

"Anyway, man," Derek changed the subject. "You gotta make buddies both in the team and not. Just keep yourself grounded, you know? It's easy to get swept up in half-a-million-plus salaries, and the intensity of the game and the season."

Matty laughed. "That show, Hockey Girls, or whatever…" It was some crappy reality TV show. He'd watched one episode before quitting.

"It's not far from the truth," Derek laughed. "What about you?"

"Nah," Matty shrugged. "I've seen what some of you guys go through." WAGs were a pain in the ass, from what he heard about. He made it a policy not to give advice, but guys still vented sometimes.

"At least hook up, though, man," Fleet encouraged. "What good's the jersey otherwise?"

They all laughed as Matty took the exit. "Where do you guys live, then?"

"You can drop us both off at mine," Derek told him, brightening up. "Man, those four hours went fast."

For you two, maybe. Trying not to think about or mention Kevin for four straight hours? Hah, *straight*. As if. "Yeah," Matty agreed anyway. He pulled into Derek's driveway and nodded. "Don't be too wild for your... wild vacation in Sudbury."

"We'll light up the town," Derek laughed, opening the door to pull his bags out. "Thanks, man." He reached forward for a fist bump, and so did Fleet.

Matty returned both fist bumps, then waved as they slammed the car doors to haul their stuff inside. Once they were inside, Matty backed down the driveway again, checking both ways before he pulled out onto the street. He rolled the windows down to enjoy a bit of fresh country air once he got to the highway again.

"Just us now, girl," he told Jasmine, laughing when she crawled through the seats to rest her head between the front seats. He let her get away with that, as long as her paws didn't touch the front seat. Now and then, he scratched her head, but he always kept a firm hand on the wheel. This far north, anything could be on the road—tractors, moose, porcupines, the works.

Luckily, he only encountered a few semis, tractors, a deer that skittered away from the road, and a few porcupines who'd already unhappily met cars before his.

Matty stopped another hour in to let Jasmine out for a

run and stretch his own legs, then climbed back in for the last leg of the journey, fresh and ready to go.

It was lonely apart from her company and his music. Even on a wonderful early summer day with the windows down and the music blasting, the silence grated on Matty after a couple hours. It would be incredible to have a best buddy to bring along with him on trips like this—not just one he walks, but one he could shoot the shit with, talk about all the hockey crap plaguing his brain, and so on.

Kevin was new and in need of a couple hockey buddies. Why not him?

Oh, yeah, *that* was why: he'd kissed Kevin like a porn star in the middle of a public park.

Matty groaned as he remembered it and rubbed his hand down his face, drumming his fingers on the wheel. Kevin had so much power over him now. He could out him to the press —first out gay major league player, that was bound to be a headline to remember.

But had Matty or Kevin initiated that kiss? It had felt a bit like being pulled into an inescapable orbit around him, gravity itself shifting towards Kevin.

He replayed the moment over and over in his head, trying to see it from different angles. It was possible Kevin was just as into Matty. He hardly dared to hope for it, but they *had* had fun hanging out that day.

Just before he reached Timmins, his tiny hometown, he got a text and pulled over to read it.

Careful, I heard there's a truck accident on the road up.

It was from Kevin.

Matty smiled, rubbing his face as he read the text a few times. Unless it was really bad, it wouldn't make news compared to 400-series highway accidents closer to the city. That meant Kevin had been specifically searching for news.

How sweet.

Matty answered slowly, thinking through what he wanted to say.

Thanks. Past the accident now nearly home. Ty for hanging out too, was fun yesterday.

Then, to stop himself fretting, he tossed the phone into his cup holder, scratched Jasmine's head, and pulled back onto the road.

Though he heard his phone go off a few times with reminder notifications, he ignored it until he pulled into his parents' driveway and finally grabbed his phone again.

You too.

That was it? Shit, was Kevin pissed? Was this something he wanted to talk about?

Matty was lousy at figuring this shit out, but there was nobody else he could go to about it. It would just have to wait a week, until he got back to town and met up with Kevin for their week of buddy training.

CHAPTER
Nine

KEVIN

ALL THINGS CONSIDERED, FLOYD WAS LOOKING PRETTY DAMN great compared to when Kevin had last seen him, mid-May. He'd seemed like a ball of nervous energy, but now he was quite pleased with himself. Why shouldn't he be? He had himself a goddamn boyfriend, some hot cop to boot.

Ugh. Kevin was going to wind up being the last single one in their group.

He held out hope, though. He'd never known Ryan—the strong, quiet carpenter type if there ever was one—to express an interest in dating. He was definitely gay, but he seemed to have other things to worry about, like his own carpentry business.

Fair enough, really. Kevin had been in that boat until he'd met Matty, who was in his own industry *and* perfect for him.

Kevin tried to shake off those thoughts as he drove to his parents' house. Even though it had only been a couple weeks since he'd last seen them for about half a day, he was looking forward to getting to stay with them properly.

"Hey, Mom and Dad. I'm home," he called as he pushed open his parents' front door.

"Kevin!" His mother was tall and broad-shouldered, a defense player in her own hockey days, and her hair was greying in elegant streaks. She was beaming as she crushed him in a hug and he laughed, hugging her back.

Then he hugged his father and clapped his back, hauling his bag into the house to let the doors close behind him.

"Welcome home," his father told him. "Come on through."

Once Kevin dropped off his bag in his old room—now the guest room, which felt weird—he headed back downstairs to chat with them.

"I'm barbecuing supper, if that's all right," his father told him. "Come on out."

Kevin followed his parents out to the porch and closed the door, grabbing a plastic deck chair to sprawl in with a can of beer. "So how are things?"

"Quiet without you and your brother in town."

Kevin's brother worked in Vancouver, so they only saw him every couple years when he flew out for holidays or special occasions like weddings. Kevin had lived in his own place, but at least in the same city until he'd moved to Toronto. It sounded like they had empty nest syndrome now.

"Aww," Kevin frowned. "Are you at least getting out and doing things?"

"Oh, all the time," his mother assured him as his dad flipped the burgers. "And I have my servant here to cook meals for me..."

"At your disposal, ma'am," his father pretended to bow, heading in to grab the vegetables.

"What about you?" his mother asked.

When his dad came out again and started putting the foil-wrapped packets on the grill, Kevin nodded. "Great. Training's been going fine—I'm a lot stronger already."

"That's great news. How about friends?"

Kevin chuckled. "Making a few of them, yeah. They're all friendly, don't worry about me."

"Good," his father concluded. "What's your training routine like? Intensive?"

"About the same as at home, really," Kevin told him. "Just, I do more of it at the gym now. One gym or another—there's my trainer's gym, and then a neighborhood gym closer to home that I go to when I don't have to head uptown to his."

"Right. So, I hear your friends are doing well."

"Yeah!" Kevin sipped his beer and shook his head. "Mm, Floyd's got a boyfriend now."

His mother laughed. "So all of you are…?"

"You can say it, Mom," Kevin teased. "We're not allergic to the word."

"Well… gay."

Kevin nodded. "Pretty much. Some of them might be bi, I dunno, but most of us have boyfriends now. Except me and Ryan."

"Think that'll change while you're out there? Toronto's a bigger city."

"Mom, don't pressure me," Kevin laughed. "I'll find someone when I find them."

"I just don't want you to be lonely," his mother said.

His father nodded in agreement with his mother's words and Kevin's heart squeezed. It was touching that his family cared so much about him, especially when he looked at some of his friends. Chase's family actively hated him, and Floyd's family seemed neglectful to the point of abuse.

Kevin knew how lucky he had it, and he appreciated it every time he came home.

He decided to be painfully honest. "I don't know," Kevin admitted. "All my buddies—well, almost all—have settled lives now, you know? Meanwhile I'm getting ready to spend five to ten years, maybe more if I'm really good, doing *this*. Is this really the right choice? I wonder about that sometimes. I can't date while I play... I don't want to be the poster boy. Cam almost was."

"Right," his mother nodded, sipping her lemonade and gazing over the back deck before she looked back at him. "And being closeted isn't really a choice?"

"If I date, I want it public. I don't want to hide him—whoever he is—" here, Kevin tried not to think about Matty when he said *him*, "—from everyone. He'd deserve to be alongside me like any WAG."

"WAG?" his dad frowned while his mother laughed.

"Wife and girlfriend," his mother supplied. "We had those too, in my league."

"Carol!" his father laughed.

Kevin grinned broadly, fetching plates for his father to serve the burgers and veggie packets. "Yeah, hockey's a lot more gay at the local level. The further up you get, the less people want to talk about it. But they will."

"You don't think they'll react badly?" his father asked with a skeptical frown.

Kevin shook his head. "There'll be consequences, sure, but... there's a lot of media attention, too. Nobody wants to be the di—uh, div deliberately boarding the newly-outed guy. And a lot of guys would accept having me on their team. Most guys get it."

"Good," his mother murmured and moved to the table,

pulling a chair out of his father's way for him to carry plates. "So you're still worried about it being the wrong choice?"

When he talked through it, Kevin had to admit… not really. There were potential downsides, but nothing he couldn't tolerate. If he dated another player, the schedule would be rough as hell, but long-distance wasn't *necessarily* fatal to a relationship.

"I think you need to trust your gut instinct," his father told him. "Don't lose touch with yourself. You've always had a good, safe head on your shoulders."

It was true—Kevin had never gotten into fights over his sexuality or been bullied like a lot of the guys he knew. Some of that was down to the older gay guys, a few years older than him, fighting their way up through the grades and teaching lessons the hard way. It wasn't just that, though. The other reason was that Kevin knew when to stay quiet and laugh along.

He hated that he knew that.

After supper, the sun slowly setting in the west, they stayed outside to play Scrabble over wine and beer, the insect repeller running at full speed. A little drunk, a little buzzed just from being home, Kevin spent every minute his parents wanted to spend with him.

Finally, when it was dark, his parents retreated indoors to an early bedtime, and Kevin stayed outside a little while longer to enjoy the clear, dark sky. The last clouds had cleared, and it was going to be a crisp, dark, *perfect* night to see the stars out here.

He missed that about Toronto—the constant glow and smog made it hard to enjoy the sights of nature.

Matty would see similar sights up in northern Ontario, where the city receded into country, farmland, mines, and scrub brush. Matty had driven home yesterday, and he hadn't addressed what had happened yet.

Kevin *had* to bring it up sometime soon. After all, Matty could well tell his new teammates about him, and he didn't want that coming out until *he* was ready for it. But surely he had more to lose, right?

He chewed his lip, then pulled his phone out for a quick text, glancing up at the first few stars starting to twinkle through the fading twilight.

How are things going?

It was just moments before he had a response.

Great. Hanging out with family tonight, staying up late with beer. Talking to my cousins and bro too.

Kevin half-smiled. That sounded idyllic, just like his own evening. And he was a family guy, staying home instead of going out with buddies.

Yeah? Sounds sweet. My bro's out in Vancouver.

LOL is that why you wanna ditch TO for it?

Nah we'd get in each other's faces.

It was true, too. They'd always grown up squabbling. Their relationship was better now that they weren't around each other in person to compete over everything.

Younger or older brother?

Kevin smiled. Matty was holding a conversation, so he wasn't completely turned off by… well, the slip in discretion. He answered quickly, wanting to keep him talking while he was here.

He's older. Works in pharmacy tech out there now, something geeky.

Yeah my bro's an engineer at the mine out here.

Kevin raised his eyebrows.

So you have parents wondering what the fuck you're doing playing hockey instead of a respectable career?

Matty's response made him laugh.

Not now that I got called up ;)

Kevin could only dream of that kind of salary. Right now, he was making enough to be comfortable, though, so he reminded himself not to get *too* greedy.

He just chuckled, then tapped his phone on his thigh. Now was the best possible time to bring up the kiss... but probably not directly. Neither of them wanted records of this.

Besides, maybe it would be better to do when he could see Matty's face in person.

Gotta go we're playing Monopoly. God help us all.

He laughed, then sent a quick answer.

Good luck. See you man.

The stars were twinkling brightly now, so he stayed out for an hour more just enjoying the sweep of bright specks across the whole horizon. When Kevin didn't hear from Matty again, he figured it was about bedtime anyway.

He wasn't waiting up for a text from a guy. No way.

CHAPTER

Ten

MATTY

"Hey, bro, gimme another one."

Matty tossed a can over the fire to his buddy, Josh. Before leaving for Toronto, he'd sold his ATV, so he'd had to double up behind Josh to get out here with him, plus Lyle and Trevor.

Their coolers loaded with hot dogs and meats, marshmallows, beer, and junk food, they'd headed out here to build a bush fire and sit around drinking and talking. It was the perfect summer afternoon, as far as he was concerned.

Even if they were lathered up in DEET-loaded bug spray and had a couple citronella candles burning around the edge of the clearing to try to keep the mosquitoes and blackflies at bay. Ugh, he didn't miss *that* part of being home.

"So, this party this weekend—you should hook up with Cindy. Girl's gotten even more fine since you've been gone." Trevor grinned at him.

That was the other part he didn't miss. God, Matty sometimes wished he'd come out to his buddies back home before he left, just to avoid shit like this. But he'd known back then how risky it was with his career plan. It was a bit too late now.

Not that he thought any of these three would tell people maliciously, but… gossip spread, especially in a town this size. He couldn't do it.

"Nah, man," Matty laughed. "I'm not gonna be home much this summer and it's even worse during game season. It's hell on relationships."

"I'm not talkin' relationships, you know what I mean," Trevor snickered while Matty and his buddies laughed.

"Naw," Matty shrugged again.

"Oh, you got something a little better back in Toronto, do you?" Lyle elbowed him and Matty punched his shoulder in return.

"Yeah, maybe," Matty laughed.

"What're Toronto girls like, anyway?"

Wrong guy to ask, buddy. Still, Matty grinned at Josh. "Oh, just fine."

After another laugh, talk turned to Trevor's new girlfriend and Matty was out of the spotlight.

Somehow, Matty had figured they all knew by now. It was like he expected to open his jacket one day and accidentally shine a giant gay signal light out of his chest, alerting everyone when he talked to hot guys. It was a stupid fear, but years of worrying about every little brush of contact with the guys around him here had left him thinking that way.

And he'd never dated chicks out here. As far as they all knew, he'd just been busy with hockey—which was true—and waiting until Toronto—which was true, but not in the way they thought. That made him a bit of a loser, but they liked him and kept him around anyway.

Matty had the weird feeling they knew after all, but they

were waiting for him to tell—that this conversation had been an excuse for him to talk. He kind of hoped he was right, because they'd accept him whenever he *did* tell the truth, but he couldn't read more into it yet.

And speaking of Kevin… Well, he hadn't been speaking or thinking directly of him, but Kevin's face kept popping into his mind every so often anyway. He was just so cute and prone to wandering through Matty's mind. He wanted to text him just to see how it was going, but there was no cell signal this far out in the bush.

Even if Kevin never wanted to kiss him again, Matty really wanted to hang out with him again. There was a kind of connection there he hadn't felt in a long time, since sneaking around in high school with Danny before he'd left for Montreal.

And then Matty had dated briefly in Toronto—a couple months here or there, largely summer flings. Still, he'd never *clicked* in the kind of way where he could talk for hours just days after meeting a guy.

Fuck. He was really smitten.

CHAPTER
Eleven

KEVIN

THE RIDE BACK TO THE AIRPORT WAS ALMOST DEPRESSING, IF Kevin really thought about it. He wasn't sure when he'd have another chance to come out. He was hoping to get out after a few camps. If he could catch another week with his parents before the weird road schedule of games, he'd be glad of that.

"Thanks for the ride, man," Kevin told Ryan. They hadn't really chatted even over the last couple days. It felt a little like he was drifting out of touch with his friends back here, but Kevin told himself that was ridiculous.

"No problem. I mean, everyone else is busy… canoodling with their boyfriends…"

Kevin snorted with laughter and grinned. "Jealous?"

"Nahhh," Ryan drawled, but he glanced sideways at Kevin. "Are you?"

He totally was, then.

"Yeah," Kevin chuckled. "It's kind of nice to see, of course… but I also hate them. It's so easy for the rest of them, huh?"

"Yeah, I guess it would be," Ryan nodded. From what

Kevin knew, Ryan wasn't fully out to his relatives, but he at least commanded respect professionally. He wouldn't lose carpentry jobs—probably—if he did come out. "Maybe a little jealous, then."

Kevin sighed. "It's not a big deal. I like focusing on work. It'd just be nice to have someone to come home to sometimes."

"Right," Ryan agreed. "I keep figuring I'll meet someone through my business, but so far, no dice. You never know, though."

"Ever consider moving out to Toronto or somewhere?" Ryan's brother was out there, so Kevin kind of figured he was hoping to.

To his surprise, Ryan shook his head. "I like it there. I mean, all the others—Cam and Noah, Jackson and Chase, Thomas and Alex, Chase and Greyson—Jesus, there's a lot of couples!" he laughed. "All the others proved it can be done."

"What can be? Living at home and meeting someone?" When Ryan nodded, Kevin nodded, too. "Ah, yeah. But there's just more to choose from out where I am. Don't write it off."

"Oh, I'm not. I'm coming to Toronto Thursday to visit my brother, maybe see the city a little," Ryan admitted.

"Really? You never said until now! Shit, man, you should crash with me." It was kind of short notice, but having a buddy out would be awesome. Everyone had promised to visit Kevin, but somehow they'd never gotten around to it yet. He figured they probably wouldn't. People were all talk and no action about that kind of stuff.

"My bro offered me an air mattress at his place, but I wanna see you for sure," Ryan told him, then punched his shoulder. "We can be the sad singles at the bar, huh?"

"Yeah," Kevin agreed with a broad smile. "That'd be nice."

Once they pulled into the airport, Ryan helped him unload his rolling suitcase and backpack, then crushed him in a quick, strong hug. "Take care of yourself, man. See you Thursday, eh? Or Friday?"

"At least one of those should work for me. You take care of yourself too." Kevin took a moment to look closely at him —he looked a little older, and though he was smiling, it wasn't hard to tell he'd been more emotional than he'd let on in the car.

Kevin felt kind of bad. He did *sort of* have someone now that Matty was around, it was just… so tentative. And from their texts, it sounded like they were meeting up tomorrow.

He might be a lot closer to dating than he was letting on to Ryan. He just didn't want to count his chickens before they hatched. He'd tell Ryan later—maybe Thursday, if everything went *really* well.

"See you, man," Kevin waved, shouldering his backpack and rolling the suitcase into the little place.

Security was almost a joke—a single lineup snaking between glass waiting rooms. He was through before he knew it, choosing from the plentiful waiting room options. He opted to go right and pick up a coffee before his plane got there.

While he did, he browsed Matty's Facebook profile. Matty had found his profile and sent a friend request yesterday—from an account with no photo and a slightly different name, no doubt to keep fans away. There wasn't a lot on his profile, but Kevin recognized a few players' names in the likes and comments on what he did have on his wall— some vacation photos, a couple action shots, and some statuses about food.

Then he came across a pro photo of Matty and paused in his scrolling, his index and middle fingers hovering over the trackpad while he took in the details: the wisps of hair across his forehead, the flush in his cheeks of a good game, his stick in his hands, one skate just slightly off the ice as he prepared to step off. And his lips slightly parted... they looked so kissable.

God, his eyes were gorgeous. The photographer had focused perfectly on them, giving the photo so much depth.

Kevin realized he was staring like a fool and closed his laptop to drink deeply from his coffee.

No ogling him until you talk, he told himself, as much as that idea made his stomach sink.

"Morning!"

"Hey," Kevin grunted back at Hans and raised his hand, finishing his text message to Matty.

Ready to work out when you are.

Then he sent it and put his phone face-down on the table before rising for a quick back-slapping hug in passing on his way to the kitchen. "Hey, man. How's it been?"

"Quiet without you around here," Hans told him.

"Still not going home this summer?" Kevin felt bad for the foreign players, with family further away. Many came from families that had resettled to Canada, but not Hans. His family had moved back to Germany a couple years ago, and he wasn't sure Hans had seen them more than a couple times since.

"Nah," Hans shrugged it off.

Kevin's phone went off and he headed back to the table with another portion of his smoothie to check it out.

Meet at the bus stop in 30?

Perfect. He answered quickly.

Yep.

"What's up?" Hans asked, and Kevin quickly glanced at him.

"Sorry. Just arranging to meet up with Matty. We're training together this week. Glenn wanted us to." He said the last bit almost apologetically. Hans probably dreamed of working with Glenn.

"Ah," Hans nodded. There was a moment of something like jealousy on his face, but he shrugged it off. "He seems to be taking you under his wing. It's good to have friends in high places. And on your own team, of course."

"Yeah," Kevin nodded. "I'm pretty lucky. Okay, I gotta finish this and then get dressed. What're you doing?"

"Nothing much. I have Final Fantasy," Hans shrugged.

"Okay. Have fun with that," Kevin laughed as he headed off to his room.

He left the house in a brisk stride, bringing his spare gym bag since most of his gear was still at Glenn's gym. Once he caught sight of Matty lingering by the bus stop, all his nervousness about seeing him again was gone.

A grin spread across Kevin's face and he raised a hand to wave while Matty waved back.

Matty pulled him in for a quick back-slapping hug. "Hey, bro! How's it going? You didn't tan at all."

"You neither!" Kevin laughed, elbowing him before leaning against the bus shelter. "Man, I saw everyone, I think. Oh, I told Cam hi from you and he said something like *hi asshole, get out here and see me.*"

Matty burst out laughing. "Oh yeah, I will if I can!" he promised. "I'll text him later. So, you ready to get ready for this camp?"

"Prospects camp?" Kevin had been trying not to think about it for the last week or more. "Sort of."

"Don't look so terrified," Matty laughed, trying to ruffle his hair. Kevin flipped him off and smacked his hand away. "It'll go fine. Man, it's just a lot of drills and people watching and telling you how to get better. They don't just want the best guys—they want guys who take direction and immediately improve."

Kevin hummed. That actually made sense. "Right," he nodded.

"And it's a great time. All the camps are," Matty shook his head. "It's stupid fun."

Kevin laughed. "Great." He climbed on the bus when it pulled on, flashing his pass and heading back to stand by the back door.

They hadn't discussed the kiss yet, but there hadn't been a good moment. He would soon.

By the time they were off the bus, they were in a friendly shoving match as they talked and tried to rustle each other's nerves.

They were half-wrestling when Kevin pulled back and held his arms up, laughing so hard he almost couldn't breathe, to signal peace so he could buzz them into the gym.

Matty grinned and winked at him, then put his own hands up before shoving them into his pockets. "You are *such* a younger brother."

"What's *that* supposed to mean?" Kevin exclaimed, his voice cracking from surprised offense.

Matty laughed loudly at that. "Nothing."

Kevin shoved him again before holding the door for him, and they headed into the gym.

This place wasn't completely filled with hockey guys, so it felt a little more private for a discussion like the one Kevin wanted to have. It occurred to him as they changed into workout gear in the locker room that it still might not be the best place, though.

The workout itself was easy compared to Glenn's, just warming them up with conventional machine exercises. Then they went through some bicep curls and deadlifts, dead simple stuff.

Then, at last, it was time to cool off again. "Conditioning while we cool off?"

"Sure," Kevin agreed to Matty's suggestion and moved over to the elliptical trainer with him, programming his machine to identical settings as Matty's.

Once they started, Kevin didn't have a lot of other places to look besides over at Matty or up at the TV. He waited for the commercial break. "Oh man. Reality TV."

He couldn't see a remote anywhere to change the channels, either. He had to talk to the gym staff about that sometime.

"Hey, I watch it sometimes," Matty snorted.

Kevin groaned. "Really?" Then, he shook his head. "Me too, though. I watched that WAG program about Toronto…"

"Okay, that program was all bullshit," Matty heatedly shook his head. "I mean, I don't know the guys on this team really well, but I knew a couple of them… we all hang out the same places, you know. And when the crew was there, everyone was acting real different."

Kevin hummed. He'd suspected as much. "But it's fun to watch."

"Yeah, that's about all it's got going, but… I'm a sucker for it, too," Matty laughed. "Especially cooking shows.

Kevin groaned and kept his voice down. "I watch cake shows! How gay is that?"

Matty eyed him for a moment and Kevin winced and held a hand up in a half-apology. But Matty shook his head slightly, telling him it was cool despite Kevin's burning hot cheeks. Matty told him, "I think any show's just as bad. It's all like junk food for the brain."

"Yeah," Kevin agreed, relieved to be let off the hook there. Sometimes he didn't like what he laughed along with, and now and then something slipped out that he privately regretted.

That would be one big advantage of coming out—less expectation to say that kind of stuff.

But he pushed that aside.

"After we're done, wanna come back to my place? Meet my roommates and Jasmine?"

"I dunno about your roommates," Kevin grinned. "But I'll meet any dog who wants to meet me."

Matty laughed, his eyes sparkling. It was a healthy look along with his glowing cheeks, and it made Kevin smile. "I like the way your head's screwed on, man."

They headed back to the locker room, still jostling each other lightly, but they were both a little too worn out to go for a headlock.

The only thing Kevin was certain of going into this discussion was that Matty wasn't *totally* uncomfortable with him.

A lot of guys would have backed off and kept two arms-length away from him forever after that kiss. But Matty hadn't. Either Matty was the coolest, most accepting guy ever, or he'd loved that kiss as much as Kevin had.

And it didn't help that every time their eyes met, there was that tense crackling second before one of them smiled or made a joke or diffused the tension. Unless Kevin was horribly wrong, his second theory could well be right.

That chemistry would be *insanely* good in bed.

Please let his roommates not be home and his dog... not be in his room.

Twelve

MATTY

AS HE STOOD UNDER THE STREAM OF HOT WATER, MATTY angled his body slightly away from Kevin's, as was polite. That didn't explain the way his heart raced every time he looked over, carefully keeping his gaze up on Kevin's face. He didn't normally have to keep his eyes up—he just naturally didn't want to see his teammates buck naked, hot or not.

That subtle difference was weird. Matty just liked Kevin, though. Kevin was nice and friendly, open, easy to be around, smarter than he gave himself credit for...

Matty just *really* wanted to be bros. Especially since Kevin seemed willing to overlook and play along with his awkward, clumsy, hella public kiss.

He kept going back and forth on why the hell he felt so weird around Kevin. Part of him knew how much leverage Kevin now had over him, but Kevin hadn't once hinted at it.

Fucking hell, this guy was willing to overlook the kiss, not even bringing it up to make him squirm from teasing embarrassment later? That made him kind of the best bro ever. Or maybe Kevin was that desperate for a buddy in the city now that he'd just moved here, which made Matty want to be friends even more.

He couldn't wait to bring him home and give him nachos and beer and introduce him to his roommates.

Matty scrubbed his pits and bits on autopilot, thanking God Kevin didn't try to talk so he didn't have to play the *your ass is in my peripheral vision* game.

Even if he wanted it to be. *Especially* because he wanted it to be.

Matty shook off his layers of thoughts, which were mostly useless bullshit speculation anyway, and stepped into his clothes. Kevin got dressed around the same time, and by the time he headed to the locker room door, Kevin was right there in his flip-flops alongside him.

"You're quick to get ready to go," Kevin told him.

"Yeah, with being the last one to leave the gym all the time," Matty laughed. "Sometimes they really wanna lock up and go. You get good at fleeing."

Kevin laughed. "I bet. You hungry?"

"Yeah. I got stuff for nachos at home, and some beer…?"

"Sold," Kevin grinned. "Bus?"

"Yep, we should make it if we jog."

The awkwardness of jogging in flip-flops made the next couple minutes fly by until they got on the bus and took their seats for the quick ride back to Matt's place.

I hope my roomies like him.

"Hey, man, you're back already. Oh, hi, Kevin." Fisher was right by the door when Kevin and Matty walked in, and he raised his hand to high-five them both. "Just worked out?"

"Hi," Kevin answered with a smile. "Yeah, it went pretty good. Glenn's routines are always intense. He had us doing deadlifts."

"Ooof, this early? God, he wants you packing on muscle," Fisher laughed. "Nice. The other guys are home, by the way."

CJ, Chris, and Fisher lived with Matty. They'd had a fifth guy in the house, Nate—their token non-hockey-player—but he wasn't home a lot over the summer. He hadn't been home much lately, in fact. It was kind of worrying, but so far, he'd been paying rent.

When they got to the living room, CJ and Chris were sprawled in front of the TV while Fisher headed to pick up a book and crash in the armchair again. Jasmine was curled on her dog bed, napping, but she got up to greet them both, too.

Matty liked that Kevin knelt to scratch her head and greet her personally.

After their rounds of greetings, Chris nodded at Kevin. "You working him too hard?" he told Matty, shaking his head. "Shame. Give the newbie a season."

"Nah, he can take it," Matty smiled, and when he elbowed Kevin, Kevin looked pleased at the praise. "He's gonna be a force to reckon with. Okay, nachos."

"Oooh, yes, please," Fisher smirked.

"Not for you, loser," Matty laughed. "I made you all pizza yesterday. You seriously ate your way through all of that?"

The three guys gave him guilty looks.

Kevin snorted with laughter. "Sometimes I'm glad my household's pretty small."

Matty and Kevin grabbed beers from the fridge, and Kevin sat at the counter while Matty got their nachos ready. They didn't say much yet, listening in on the conversation in the living room—some gossip about the Zamboni driver at the local rink, and the running inside joke that he was actually an alien trying to infiltrate Canada from the least suspicious possible position.

Then, conversation turned to their weekend getaway.

"So are we doing this cabin thing or not?" CJ asked, crinkling his beer can and tossing it in the bin near the kitchen doorway.

Matty poked his head out. "Not at my parents' cabin, that's a hell of a long way away. Let's get a cabin closer."

"Yeah," Chris agreed. "Not like we can't afford it, splitting it a bunch of ways for just a weekend."

Matty glanced at Kevin, who was looking away like he didn't want to intrude or invite himself along. Idiot, of course he was getting invited. He elbowed Kevin. "Hey, you're coming, too, right?"

Kevin looked surprised. "Yeah? I mean, yeah, thanks. Sure," he nodded, his shoulders sinking in relief.

Hans wasn't Matty's favorite player—something had always been up with him, but Matty had never been able to figure out where his gut instinct came from. Still, he had nothing personally against the guy, so he shrugged. "You bringing Hans, too?" It seemed like a good idea to befriend Kevin's friends, too, no matter what this weird *thing* turned out to be between them.

"I'll ask him," Kevin smiled, then nodded. "Thanks."

"No problem. Hey, you wanna choose the next movie? They all have horrible taste."

CJ groaned and Chris threw the remote at Matty's head, so he snatched it out of the air and smacked Chris's arm with it before handing it to Kevin.

As they settled down to shoot the shit while superhero movies played in the background, Matty relaxed and sprawled along the floor by the coffee table, watching Kevin relax equally.

This wasn't the intimate kind of getting-to-know-you he half-wanted with Kevin, but they had to establish a lot of things first. For now, that had to stay a kinda kinky, embarrassing fantasy.

Kevin finally told them he had to head out and shop for groceries, and Matty saw him to the door. Very aware of his roommates so close by, Matty reached out for an enthusiastic back-clap and handshake before waving goodbye.

The room seemed a little duller without Kevin in it. The moment Matty sat down again, Fisher looked at him. "God, it's about time you socialized with someone other than us. You were becoming a hermit."

Matty snorted. "Was not, shut up."

"You sort of were," CJ smirked. "But he's a cool kid. Reminds me a little of Cam. I can see how they got along well."

"Yeah," Matty agreed. "He wants me to visit, too. I'll have to try to get back this summer before the preseason starts."

"Shhh, it's just getting to the good bit."

Kissing, of course, with the obligatory hot woman. Matty rolled his eyes at the movie, but his buddies were into it, so he didn't comment. They all expected that kind of commentary from him anyway.

Though he often spoke too suddenly and loudly, he also called out a little more shit than guys wanted to hear, so he tried to keep it toned down around the guys he knew were cool.

He couldn't resist sneaking in one comment. "Of *course* she's gonna be kidnapped next scene so he can swoop in and save her. Princess Peach there."

"Shhh," CJ kicked him.

"Losers," Matty laughed, getting up in the middle of the kissing scene. He gathered empty beer cans to drop into the recycling by the kitchen doorway on the way to get another beer. If they were swapping looks behind his back, he didn't wanna know.

CHAPTER
Thirteen

KEVIN

Just as Kevin finished his morning push-ups and rewarded himself with a box of Smarties, Hans wandered into the kitchen. He was shirtless and in just his lounge pants, but there was zero appeal there. Unlike Matty, who could be fully-dressed and Kevin still always wanted to see him in less.

Somehow, every thought he had seemed to relate to Matty these days. Kevin resisted the urge to groan at himself.

"Morning."

"Hey," Hans answered, eyeing the chocolate. "That allowed?"

"Fuck off, they can't control me… until next week." Kevin grinned and dumped the rest of the candies in his mouth. They clicked and rattled around his teeth as he crunched through mouthfuls of hard candy shells and soft chocolate interiors.

"Where are you off to?"

Kevin raised his brows and pointed at his mouth. "Gwrfn aught wo mae."

"Gross, dude," Hans laughed and passed him to grab coffee.

Once Kevin swallowed, he answered, "Working out with Matty. You wanna come?"

"Nah."

"Suit yourself," Kevin shrugged, picking shell crumbs out of his teeth. "We're off to the gym. Catch you later." He grabbed his spare gym bag again, heading back to the bus stop to meet Matty.

It was weird, with Hans. He had less money, so he often complained he couldn't keep up with Kevin's training routine, making that a sensitive subject. But he was a member of this same neighborhood gym. He could come along on these sessions and let Kevin pass along what he'd learned. He just… didn't. Far be it from Kevin to judge, but he seemed to be more interested in video games all summer.

Matty was leaning against the bus stop, and shit, he was hot. He had one foot up, the sole of his shoe pressed against the bus stop glass. His thumbs were hooked in his pockets as he gazed off sideways across the street. White cords led up to his ears, and his bright teal t-shirt with a yellow print drew eyes.

It looked great on him, though.

"Hey." Kevin waved sideways to catch Matty's peripheral vision and laughed when he jumped. "Lost track of time?"

"I did there," Matty admitted, laughing and pushing himself away from the bus stop. He adjusted his gym bag to the other arm and yanked out his earbuds, bundling them into his pocket. "Got here a little early."

"Early? This time of day?" Kevin teased. "I like your commitment."

Matty grinned, then turned to keep an eye down the

street for the bus. "Ready to get big and hard today?" He threw a wink over his shoulder.

Kevin snorted with laughter. "At least one of those things." He didn't look away, though.

Then Matty glanced back down the street. "Here's the bus."

Fuck, are we just not gonna talk about it? Apparently not.

Kevin followed Matty onto the bus and hung onto the pole for the short trip to Patson's Gym. This early in the morning, they might be lucky enough to have the gym—or one room of it—to themselves, at least.

They changed quickly into gym clothes once they hit the locker room, not saying much else. The companionable silence was something else Kevin liked, though.

After warmups, they moved to one of the weight rooms, which was usually quiet. This time of day, it was dead and would be until afternoon when the business guys who lived around here started getting off work. If any other players were there, not many of them were doing weights this time of year. It was their own little world where they got to practice bicep curls and make fun of each other's toe raises.

"Okay, now for Glenn's shit," Matty told Kevin. "He wants us doing core strength exercises, too. We've been avoiding them."

Kevin didn't want to do the stupid sit-ups and planks and crap. They were boring in comparison to free weights, or the drills they'd be running next week. But if Glenn assigned them, there was a reason.

He groaned, then dropped to his knees on the mat in front of the mirror. "Fine."

There was a moment where Matty stayed standing and Kevin glanced up at him, then became suddenly hyperaware that Matty was standing right by him, his crotch at eye-level.

Matty was suddenly sinking to his knees, looking everywhere but Kevin as he rolled onto his ass to assume a sit-up position.

That was interesting. Maybe he was feeling the same kind of click between them.

Kevin automatically shifted to grab Matty's ankles and hold his feet down as Matty folded his hands behind his neck and started crunching.

Matty's hair was all out of place again, his face already glowing with exertion. He got red so easily, which Kevin found adorable.

Whoa, that's a weird choice. Kinda cute, Kevin corrected himself.

Each time Matty's chest brushed his thighs, that brought him just inches away from Kevin, who was crouched by his feet.

And then Kevin's mind wandered back to a certain gif he'd seen online—a looping video of a guy sitting up, almost exactly like Matty was doing right now, and kissing another guy every time he came up.

Kevin's cheeks were instantly hot.

"What?" Matty laughed, his voice a breathless half-tone from exertion. His eyes were crinkled in amusement.

Kevin shook his head. "Nothin'," he tried to drawl, but Matty wasn't letting it go.

"Whaaat?"

"It's pretty gay," Kevin snorted with laughter, smirking playfully at Matty lowering himself to the mat. The word didn't mean anything. They were just horsing around... like guys did.

Matty sat up again, but this time, he didn't stop short of his knees. He leaned up and in, quickly pressing his lips against Kevin's. His lips were warm and smooth and... oh, Jesus, kissable.

Kevin's chest was hotter than his cheeks, his fingers itching with the urge to pull apart Matty's ankles and scoot up close to him and kiss the *fuck* out of him...

"This gay?" Matty teased, his breath warm on Kevin's lips. His eyes were open, focused on Kevin's despite their short distance.

Kevin was still almost breathless as he wrinkled his nose. "That's pretty gay, dude," he laughed, but he didn't pull back.

He didn't necessarily want to discourage Matty. Plus, if it was a game of gay chicken, backing out first would make him the fucking loser here, and he didn't do losing.

And maybe Matty *wasn't* just kidding around.

Kissing once? That was kind of a big thing, even if it was so short a kiss it might as well have been a Quebecer's "see you tomorrow" kiss.

Kissing twice?

There was something here. Kevin just couldn't put his finger on it, but boy, did he want to.

Matty's lips were moving—counting down to ten to the end of his rest break, Kevin realized as soon as Matty lay back again.

On the tenth sit-up, this time, Kevin leaned in impulsively across Matty's knees, his hands still tight on Matty's ankles, to kiss him open-mouthed.

Matty's chest was heaving for breath, but he kissed back hard, their lips and tongues mashing in a quick, fierce spilling over of whatever the fuck they were holding back around each other. Kevin was positive Matty could hear the pounding of his heart, even if he wasn't the one working out right now.

The sexy fuckin' sound of kissing and heaving breath was all they could hear, though Kevin was so wound-up he was a coil about to snap from listening to the hallway.

Matty sucked Kevin's bottom lip and swiped his tongue across it, and then Kevin slid his tongue against Matty's lips, teasing at the tip of Matty's tongue and licking his way into his mouth…

Then, he pulled back abruptly, so fucking sure he'd heard footsteps. His lips were flushed and his cheeks probably were, too.

Matty was watching him, the tension in his face nothing Kevin had ever seen from guys fucking around with him like guys did.

He was worried—scared, even—about Kevin's response.

So Kevin just winked. "More like *that* gay," he told Matty, who cracked up laughing.

"Your face is—" Matty started, and Kevin let go of his ankles, sending him lurching backwards. "Hey!"

Kevin grinned. "Sorry," he pretended to apologize.

"Your turn then, loser," Matty shoved Kevin, and then…

They were both laughing. Kevin was flat on his back on the mat, Matty kneeling by his side above him. The light behind and above Matty made his blond hairs glow, his face bright and teasing and ruddy red from his sit-ups. His lips were still wet from their kisses.

And Kevin was *not* going to get a boner, he just wasn't— not in the middle of the gym, please…

Those were definitely footsteps.

Kevin pulled his feet towards him and pressed them hard

into the ground, blocking his view of Matty with his knees as he laced his fingers behind his head.

Whoa, that wasn't helping. Matty's fingers were around his ankles, holding him down. Almost boner material right there, let alone everything else that had just happened. Kevin pulled himself up into a first, sloppy sit-up. His form was terrible, but whatever. It would give his cock a little time to settle the *fuck* down against his thigh, thanks very much.

By the second or third sit-up, he'd pulled his spine straight, and he had a quick glance over.

Hans was rounding the corner of the doorway, looking first into the room across the hall, then into theirs. "Ah, there you are. Hey."

Kevin's heart sank. That was the end of their flirtation for the day, then. "Thought you weren't coming!" He flopped back on the mat to look up and over in his direction.

"Nah, me too. But it wouldn't kill me to get on the machines once in a while, I figured," Hans shrugged, his gaze flickering between the two of them. "Hey, Matty."

"Hey."

Kevin watched Hans move over to the hip abductor. When his gaze returned to Matty, Matty gave him a quick nod, but that playful rogue was gone. This was all-business Matty, working out like it was his job.

Which it was—for both of them. Sure, he got enough time off in the summer to handle all his adult life affairs like dentistry and taxes, and see his buddies when they flew into Toronto, but he still had to stay fit.

Kevin restarted his sit-up count at zero.

Once they were done with sit-ups, they planked for as long as they could handle, then moved over to the yoga mats to stretch.

None of them said anything yet. The weights clanked up and down on Hans's machine as he grunted through his exertion, and Kevin and Matty's joints cracked now and then as they stretched out their bodies from head to toe.

A couple minutes later, Hans exhaled an audible, "Whew." He was leaning back on the bench, taking a moment's breather.

Oh, yeah. Now that Hans was around, Kevin remembered the other thing he didn't *really* wanna ask his roommate, but he should. "Hey, Hans. Dude, Matty and a couple of his buddies and I are going to a cabin this weekend." He glanced at Matty to confirm the invitation was still sound. "You wanna come?"

"Yeah," Matty chimed in. "If you want, there's room for one more."

When Kevin twisted around for a look, Hans was sitting up and wiping his forehead. "Nah, man. I'm meeting up with a bunch of our team to practice this weekend. Last weekend before camp, ya know? Thanks, though."

"Yeah, yeah, that's cool," Matty waved it off. "Just thought I'd offer, man."

"Thanks, man," Hans automatically answered.

Kevin's body ached as he slowly pushed himself to his feet. "Well, Jesus fuck, b'ys, that's it for me."

Matty burst out laughing. "You going Newfie on us now? You from there?"

"No, no," Kevin laughed. "But I got a buddy or two who's rubbed off on me."

And by buddies, he meant his ex-boyfriend, who'd gone to university out in St. John's. Their last year had been long-distance, and on the rare occasions they'd gotten a chance to get together...

Yeah, he *had* rubbed off on him.

Kevin's cheeks were hot again as he strode for the weight room door. "See you, Hans. Be home later, maybe after supper."

"Kay," Hans answered bluntly, his voice short as he hauled down on the pulleys he tightly gripped, his breath coming in quick pants. "See you."

Matty raised a hand and followed after Kevin to the locker room.

With a couple other guys around, Kevin didn't dare make a move on Matty in the shower, even teasingly, to try to get a feel for his chances.

Instead, he waited until they were dressed and strolling through the gym lobby.

"I gotta split today," Kevin told Matty with a reluctant smile. "Gotta get my teeth fixed up."

"Yeah? I did that a couple weeks back, and I'm doing taxes now," Matty laughed. "God, our lives are weird."

"It's our own calendar," Kevin agreed, holding the gym door open for Matty as they stepped out onto the sidewalk and walked to the bus stop. "Spring cleaning happens in summer."

Matty snorted with laughter. "Nicely put. Okay, I'm grabbing a bus here."

"I'm heading off that way."

"Cool. Okay."

There was a moment there that they hadn't had with Matty's roommates around. Kevin honestly wasn't sure whether to go for a back-slap, a handshake, a hug…

…Or a kiss.

Matty's eyes flicked down to Kevin's lips.

But no fucking way. Not in front of the gym, with Hans

around and probably other players. And a couple people waiting at the bus stop here, some stepping forward towards the curb.

Kevin glanced down the road—the bus was approaching.

When he looked back at Matty, the moment was gone and Matty just slapped his shoulder. "Good luck with your teeth, man. They look all right, though."

"Thanks." Kevin laughed at the weird compliment, but he'd take it.

"I'll give 'em something to do if you like." Matty pretended to punch him in the mouth like they were on the ice and the gloves were off.

Kevin laughed and shoved him off him, so Matty shoved back, and Kevin braced himself.

Oh, my God. We're like teenage boys.

The bus was slowing down now, so Kevin just leaned in for a quick half-hug. "Catch you later. I got a buddy visiting tomorrow, so I might bring him along."

"Cool," Matty smiled, but there was a flicker there —disappointment?

Shit. Maybe he wanted to *properly* make out.

They could make time for that… and space. Kevin would find a way. Kick Hans out? Invade Matty's place until all his roommates were out? If Matty said the word…

But instead, Matty raised a hand and stepped onto the bus, and Kevin was left watching after him like a forlorn lover.

Fuuuck. Fuck, fuck, fuck. He wants to be alone with me.

Kevin couldn't handle the way that made his heart hammer with joy.

CHAPTER

Fourteen

RYAN

As much as Ryan complained about his little brother's choice of city—he worked as a realtor in downtown Toronto now—he had to admit, Eric had a pretty sweet place. Only problem was, he was usually working too much to enjoy it.

Ryan had chosen the complete opposite career path when he went into the trades. He'd always enjoyed working with his hands and building stuff, and when he figured out that there'd always be a demand for those services, it was a no-brainer.

Now that he was out of his apprenticeship and working on his own on building sites, his own job sucked up a little more time than he'd thought, but he couldn't complain about his wages. And he still built things at home for fun, and sometimes to sell on the side. He'd taken a long weekend to see his brother here, but Eric had to work today.

Luckily, Kevin lived here now and had instantly agreed to pick him up, show him to Eric's place as long as Ryan knew the address, and hang out that afternoon before his brother was off in the evening. Apparently Kevin was off to the cabin with some friends this weekend, but at least they'd catch each other today.

"Hey!"

Ryan glanced around until he located Kevin's cheery grin, then laughed as he moved in for a quick hug by the luggage carousel. "Hey, man. How's it going? Long time no see," he joked.

"Nah, it's like I saw you last week," Kevin grinned. He looked good, though. Even more than last week, Kevin was glowing with life.

They were all happy for him, that he'd gotten his dream job out here. Well, one league down from his *dream* job, but still a comfortable one. But was there more than a job going on here? Kevin looked… bright.

Ryan usually didn't say much. He was a lot happier to let everyone else do the talking while he just watched and listened. He picked up a lot that way. "You're looking happy," he commented, though, unable to resist.

"Yeah. Almost training week," Kevin laughed. "And I'm where I wanted to be, training-wise."

"Great," Ryan approved. He kept an eye out for his suit-case, and once it passed by, he grabbed it. "Where we headed?"

"Over to the ferry, then a streetcar. You got your brother's address?"

"I'll text you it."

They pulled out their phones for the silent exchange, and then Kevin squinted at his phone. "Ohhh yeah. Okay, no problem, that's close."

"It looked like it on the map." Ryan still wasn't too familiar with Toronto. He'd only been out here on vacation a couple times as a kid, and to visit his brother a few times. He didn't really leave Fredericton much, honestly.

Walking through downtown Toronto was a little overwhelming for Ryan. Crowds were in general, actually. He stayed close to Kevin as they headed over to the ferry bridge, then boarded the boat.

"So, how's it been going with everyone?" Kevin asked.

"In the last week?" Ryan laughed.

"Just in general." Kevin cleared his throat as he leaned on the railing, glancing out across the Toronto harbor. "Feels like everyone's on the other side of the world sometimes."

Ryan winced in sympathy, casting his mind around their group of friends for things Kevin wouldn't have heard. "Let's see... oh. Oh, Jesus, that's right." His big news of the week—but could he share it?

Nah, Noah wouldn't mind.

"What? What is it?" Kevin pressed, picking up on Ryan's excitement.

"I'm making a custom ring box for someone..."

Kevin's eyes went huge. "No shit. Who?" he exclaimed. The way his face worked, he was running through the possibilities.

Ryan almost laughed at the look on his face. "Noah."

"No *shit*," Kevin breathed out, and Ryan did laugh this time. Kevin was clearly both delighted and shocked. "He's proposing? When?" His voice almost cracked from excitement.

Ryan snorted with laughter. "I don't know, man, he won't tell me. He just said this summer."

"Oh my God, that's... that's so cool," Kevin laughed. "Wow. Christ. I guess they're an item now, then."

"They all are." Ryan tried not to sound jealous. The doors

were closing, the ferry almost on the move. "I mean, most of us are getting really… settled in."

"Except you, obviously."

"And you," Ryan returned, but watched Kevin closely. "I assume."

There was a second of hesitation from Kevin that said more than his following words. "What? Yeah, I mean. Uh… well…"

Aha. Ryan smiled slightly and let him talk.

"I mean, there's someone I like," Kevin admitted after a long few seconds of contemplation. "But shit, it could get complicated."

Ryan was curious, but not if Kevin wasn't ready to share yet. "Yeah?"

"Yeah." Nope, not ready to talk, then. "Hey, you wanna come to a practice later this summer or something? You coming out again this year?"

"I thought I did that a couple years back," Ryan smirked.

Kevin groaned but chuckled. Any coming-out joke mandated at least a chuckle from their little group of friends —tight-knit enough to be family by now, even the ones not apparently marrying soon.

"I was thinking this fall, actually. Cam wants to come out to see all his old buddies on the team, and watch one of your home games. Especially you and Matty."

Kevin jolted slightly. "Oh yeah! Of course."

"You met him already, didn't you?" Ryan asked. "Seem like a nice guy?"

"Well, if he's friends with Cam," Kevin shrugged, and Ryan had to agree. Cam was a pretty good judge of character about everything except his boyfriends. Thank God he'd lucked into meeting Noah. "But yeah, he's cool. We're working out together. Glenn wanted us together because we both have the same work ethic."

"Obsessive gym nerds, then," Ryan teased. It wasn't like he never hit the gym himself, but most of his tone came from hauling lumber and shit around, not daintily pressing on machines.

Kevin laughed sheepishly. "Pretty much. Man, good to have you out, though. We'll grab lunch as soon as you drop your stuff off at your brother's, and then... the gym?"

"That sounds great."

Ryan smiled out across the harbor as the ferry coasted to the city shore. If he only had a couple days in Toronto, he was gonna make the most of them. And maybe spy on Kevin a little, like everyone back home wanted him to do.

"Oh, Jesus."

It was only half an hour into their gym workout and Ryan regretted making fun of Kevin's weight machines.

It wasn't like he couldn't handle the weight—Kevin was being careful not to get him hurt. But this was just a different kind of pull. Or, in this case, push, since he was lying flat on his back, raising a weighted machine board with his feet.

Kevin laughed as he hovered nearby, ready to spot him if his knees gave way. "Almost there. Don't stop. Push harder."

"Jesus, go get laid," Ryan laughed, rolling his head back as he slowly raised and lowered his feet again, starting to count backwards in his last set.

"You too, you dick," Kevin snorted with laughter. "Oh come on, you can go harder than—don't. Dude, don't make it weird." But Kevin was laughing loudly now, covering his face with his hand.

Ryan tried to keep his breathless laughs under control until he got that last painful raise and lower out of the way, then locked the bar and lay back on the bench for a hearty, quick laugh. "You said it, not me."

"Did I pass the test, then?" Ryan slowly sat up, ignoring the burn in his calves.

"With mediocre colors," Kevin smirked and came around the machine.

Ryan flipped him off. "You come lift a load of lumber out of a truck bed and see how far you get."

"No thanks." Kevin ran a hand back through his hair and chose the machine next to him, setting it up for chest work instead. "Speaking of, how's work going?"

"Good." Ryan figured he should elaborate a little more. "Just finished roughing out a new place. By the time I'm back we'll probably be on to the next house. The growth in town is crazy. You saw all those new suburbs and developments going up."

"Yeah! God, you must be up to your eyeballs in work."

Ryan laughed. That was pretty accurate, actually. "This summer's gonna be nuts. But I was thinking more about doing custom stuff, too… I don't wanna be tied completely to builders. They can go bankrupt or stop developing or whatever. And I like piecework… it's relaxing."

"You go home after a long day of sawing shit and you go saw shit for fun?"

"Hammer shit together, or sand it, or varnish it…" Ryan trailed off, then snorted. "Yeah, okay, fine."

Kevin chuckled. "No, that's cool, though." Ryan moved

around to spot him as he lay back on the bench and gripped the bar. "You're thinking you might sell some of your stuff?"

Ryan nodded. "I mean, Noah came to me about the ring box... I've been doing stuff like trunks, coat racks, all kinds of weird little things. It's actually been a lot of fun," he admitted.

"You're good, too. You can sell your stuff no problem," Kevin told him.

The praise made Ryan smile, though he knew Kevin was right. He took pride in the job he did. "At farmer's markets?"

"Why not? Cam's boss does great," Kevin shrugged. Cam worked for his soon-to-be fiancé Noah's uncle at an apiary, and according to their story, they'd first met when Cam bought some of Noah's honey. Of course, everyone had had to heckle them about *that*, but they insisted it wasn't a euphemism.

"Yeah..." Ryan trailed off, dubiously. "They got a couple carpenters there already."

"So? You can sell at Christmas fairs, too," Kevin told him. "People go apeshit for real, handmade gifts. Especially as good as your stuff is. And at least one of the farmer's markets will take you, guaranteed. I bet if Noah's uncle puts in a good word for you..."

"All right, all right," Ryan laughed. "I'm thinking about it. Just, I won't have time this summer—or probably even the fall or winter." With the ground frozen and nigh-impossible to excavate for new foundations, that was the season for interior work. "Not to work for other people, then come home and do stuff, and then somehow find time to advertise and sell it..."

Kevin blew out a breath as he carefully put the bar back

down, then stretched out and rested. "Ooof. Hmm… You could hire someone."

"Like, to build for me?"

"Nah, to do all the other shit," Kevin shrugged. "Stick to the stuff you know and like."

"Now you're a business consultant?" Ryan laughed.

Kevin slipped out from under the rack and winked. "I'll charge you for my advice unless you take it."

"*Unless?*" Ryan laughed. Clever little bastard. "Yeah, yeah," he waved him off.

Kevin slapped his shoulder, then turned. "Oh, hey, Hans."

A light-haired guy in the back corner nodded at them both, his eyes flicking to Ryan. Ryan wasn't sure he liked him—even though the guy had no reason to *dis*like him. That was kinda weird.

"Hans, this is my buddy from Fredericton, Ryan. Ryan, my roommate."

Oh yeah, that was where he'd heard the name. Ryan smiled and jerked his head in a quick upnod. "Hey, man."

"Hey." Hans glanced between them, and now Ryan's suspicion about what he was thinking was confirmed. "This your buddy?" His accent was German.

"Yeah, my buddy." Either Kevin didn't notice what he was implying by asking again, or he didn't give a shit. Ryan noticed and he didn't appreciate it, though.

"Cool," Hans concluded simply.

Ryan nodded back at Hans, then stepped out of the room to head for the locker room while Kevin had a word with his roommate.

Now he could see one of the potential complications Kevin had hinted at.

But you can't let everyone around you stop you from living your life, man.

Ryan tried to ignore the sinking recognition in his own stomach. It was always easier to see things in other people than himself.

Time to hit the shower and head for food with Kevin. They still had an afternoon to enjoy—platonically, whatever Hans thought—before Eric was off work and ready to hang out. Hopefully Hans wasn't around, because Ryan planned to enjoy it.

Fifteen

MATTY

"You ready for the weekend?"

"Oh, yeah." Kevin slammed his gym locker shut and turned to face Matty, beaming at him. He looked like he hadn't gone to a cabin with buddies... well, ever. "I'm all packed." He slung his gym bag over his shoulder, and they strolled out of the locker room towards the bus stop for the quick ride down the street.

"Aren't you an eager beaver?" Matty teased, which made Kevin crack up. He liked making Kevin laugh, though. "I'll swing by your place to pick you up at like eleven." He didn't like driving downtown in Toronto, but going out of the city was fine.

"Eleven? Okay, cool."

They still hadn't talked about the damn kisses—any of them. Matty had to catch Kevin alone sometime this weekend. It was gonna be a bit awkward being like "do you wanna kiss me again or were you just fucking with me?", but it was better than leaving it unspoken and continuing to make out unexpectedly in public.

When they went their separate ways, Matty clapped Kevin's back and half-hugged him, which was all they seemed to be goddamn doing these days. "See you in a bit."

"Later, man!"

By the time he got home, Matty had *almost* stopped thinking of what it would be like to casually kiss Kevin goodbye. He pushed the front door open, trying hard to stop thinking about Kevin's cute little smile and the way he watched him with bright, attentive eyes when he modeled the exercises the way Glenn wanted them to do them, and…

"Hey, Matty." From a quick glance at the pile of shoes by the door, everyone else was out, but that was Fisher's voice. "I made lunch."

"Sweet, thanks, man. Did you get the meat?"

"I sure did. Did you?"

Matty's eyes widened as he came around the living room corner. Fisher was grinning broadly. "What the fuck, man?" Matty exclaimed with a laugh, slapping Fisher's stomach on the way by.

"Ooooh. Sorry," Fisher snickered. "But you're ditching us for him a lot lately." But from the way he said it casually, he didn't seem to be *actually* asking the question underneath that. "Have you finally replaced Cam?"

Matty rolled his eyes. There was no *replacing* Cam, obviously. CJ and Fisher were probably best buds the same way he and Cam had been. But then Cam had to go get himself a heart condition and move to the Maritimes. Sure, he had plenty of buddies around the teams, but there was nothing like having a guy you shared all those midnight wings and six AM practices with.

"Maybe. Glenn was right, he works hard."

"Good," Fisher approved and pulled open the fridge to

start loading up the cooler with beer while Matty sat at the kitchen table to wolf down the pasta Fisher had made.

Fisher's first name was Fox, but he hated it so much he'd get aggressive when anyone said it, so they all just knew him by his last name. A lot of people didn't even know his real first name. It was like that in hockey sometimes—guys got slapped with dumb nicknames, or there was already a Matt or Chris around, so they had to go by Matty or CJ.

It was weird they didn't have any Kevins around besides this one. Matty knew a few Kevins around his age. None of them had made it up to this level in the last few years, though.

"Speaking of Cam, I wanna go to Fredericton and surprise him later this summer. Since he can't make it out during bee season," Matty said.

Fisher laughed. "Bee season."

"It is," Matty laughed. "Until, like, fall."

"Right." Fisher closed the cooler with a thud and stepped on it to click it shut, then pulled open cupboard doors. "You're so bereft without him."

Matty snorted. "Shut up, Mr. *I'm gonna cook for CJ's turn every week instead of making him learn for his damn self.*" He brandished his fork at Fisher. "Bereft?" Matty added after a moment. "That's a fancy word for you."

Fisher pretended to throw the marshmallow package at Matty's head and Matty grinned. "Whatever," Fisher told him. "I meant as a friend. You *know* what I meant."

"What, unlike you and CJ?" Matty cleaned his bowl out with bread, then finished that off, too, and downed a few gulps of pop. "When's the wedding?"

Fisher laughed again, louder this time, and rummaged for

their stash of s'mores chocolate bars. "We'll have a joint wedding with you and new guy. Kevin."

"Perfect. Cam can be our flower girl."

Fisher laughed. "What's his boyfriend's name? Noah?"

"Yeah, that's the one."

"He'll be the ring bearer, then. Perfect. Now we just need someone who doesn't suck on piano."

Matty scrunched up his face in thought as he washed up his lunch dishes. "Or guitar. Drums…?"

"Rock band: wedding edition."

"Yeah," Matty laughed, drying off his hands. "Don't mention it to Kevin 'till I get a chance to propose, though. Might be awkward." He headed upstairs to pack.

"You got it, man," Fisher called out after him.

Matty tried hard not to admit to himself that his heart was thudding at the thought. He'd had a dozen conversations like this over the last few years. Bromances were dime-a-dozen here.

It was completely fucking normal.

His glow of nervous excitement about this guy he barely knew yet, he'd locked lips with maybe three times?

That really wasn't.

"Hey, Kev!" Matty rolled down the window as he pulled up in front of Kevin's building. "You want backseat or front?"

"Hey!" Fisher protested. He'd already claimed dibs on the front seat. "I'm shotgun."

Kevin laughed. "That's fine. I can take backseat."

Chris slid over into the middle, next to CJ, leaving room for Kevin in the third seat. Poor Jasmine was sprawled across

CJ's lap, but she didn't mind. "We won't even make you go in the middle."

"O ho ho," CJ loudly laughed. He was quickly joined by the other guys, even Matty and Kevin.

Matty pretended he didn't see the flush on Kevin's cheeks as he opened the back to throw his bag in, then came around the side.

Then, Matty double-checked that the door light was off and everyone was belted in and they were off to the races.

"How's it going?" CJ asked, leaning forward to see Kevin around Chris.

"Not bad," Kevin told them. "Just talked to my parents on the phone. They're missing me already."

"Oof. Wait for the season," Fisher winced.

Kevin chuckled. "Everyone keeps saying that."

"It's pretty hard," Matty chimed in, glancing to Kevin in the rearview mirror. "But it's not *that* bad, as long as you're emailing or sending videos or whatever. Time zones are really the worst part. Especially being three hours away—four for you—when that happens."

Kevin nodded. "Can't wait for prospect camp, though. They start off with medicals, right?"

The rest of the car was eager to tell Kevin all about what to expect, from the medical to drills and expectations. Matty stayed quiet to focus on getting them out of downtown and onto the 400 north to Georgian Bay.

By the time the Toronto skyline fell around them into massive subdivisions, then housing co-ops, then flat fields and the long, straight stretch north, they were discussing pizza places.

"No, you're crazy," Kevin scoffed. "That's the *worst* delivery I've had yet."

"Which place did you call? You never call the downtown one."

"Oh, shit," Kevin exclaimed. "Really? All franchises are supposed to be the same. That's the point of a franchise."

"Yeah, well, they aren't," CJ laughed. "You'll learn real fast."

Matty smiled to himself, staying out of the conversation for now. It was just nice to hear Kevin getting along fine with the rest of them already.

Not that he'd expected any less. Kevin was easy to get along with, and so were the rest of his buddies.

The lake closed in on the left before long, peeking through gaps in trees. Matty kept a close eye out for their exit, then the dirt road they had to follow down to the dock.

The owner had left the keys for the boat and the house in a steel lockbox. Matty punched in the code and grabbed the keys, then went to pick up his own bag from the back while the guys grabbed theirs, plus the coolers and supplies. He'd had his boating license for years, so the owners were happy to let them have it without a lesson as long as they paid a deposit.

"It's not that far away, really," CJ was marveling. It had only been a couple hours' drive from Toronto, and the time had flown by.

"No, this is super-close. I wish my parents were this close," Matty laughed.

"Me too," Kevin said, which made Matty feel instantly guilty. At least he *could* drive out to see his own family over the weekend if he had a really bad week. Kevin brushed it off by grinning across the lake, though. "Holy shit, we got great weather."

It was supposed to be clear all weekend, with maybe some

cloudy patches one evening, but no rain. That was fine by Matty.

"Yeah," Chris cheered. "C'mon, someone, grab the other end of this."

Between them, they carted their stuff down to the boat, got it started, and piled in. They tried to stay more or less balanced, keeping about half of them on each side of the boat. Kevin seemed like he had good sea legs, but CJ stayed sitting down firmly as Matty gradually pushed the throttle.

It didn't have a strong engine, but it was good enough to get them over the water towards the dock and the blue-sided lake house looming into view beyond.

Matty relaxed as he approached the dock at a careful putter, steering into it until someone could hop ashore and moor the boat.

The cabin looked beautiful even from the outside, they had lots of food, and they had a whole weekend to themselves. As long as he didn't kiss Kevin in front of everyone, it was gonna be just fine.

Sixteen

KEVIN

"I GOT THIS LAST ONE."

What the hell did they need three coolers this size for, anyway? Kevin assumed they had an insane stash of beer in at least one of them. Even with his strength, it was hard to heft, which meant they had ice in it too.

Kevin hauled it up the short staircase to the deck—one of this place's two decks—and through the open sliding glass door.

"May as well leave this one in the corner. Save the fridge for food, leave the beer in the coolers?" CJ suggested, but nobody was really listening. Chris was exploring the living room while Fisher was glued to the glass windows wrapping around to show an almost 180-degree view of the lake and Matty was trying to find the wi-fi password.

"Sounds good," Kevin approved of CJ's plan. "Jesus, does this one only have beer?"

"Yeah," CJ laughed. "There's five of us, man."

"Yeah, good point."

CJ grabbed his bag and Fisher's, and Kevin recognized

the signs of a bedroom scuffle. He eyed the other guys and picked up his own backpack again.

Then CJ was off like a shot for the staircase with an unashamed little boy's grin. "Dibs on the biggest room!"

"Oh, fuck," Matty exclaimed, putting down the router and trying to step out from behind the TV. "Not fair, you asshole."

Kevin smirked and trotted upstairs after CJ. While CJ turned left, he went right towards the door at the end of the hall.

As soon as he pushed it open, he was sold.

"Whoa," he breathed out, gazing around the room. There were two single beds, but more importantly, a whole bank of windows overlooked the lake—as every window in this place seemed to, since there weren't many trees on this little island. The wall was practically glass.

Kevin dropped his backpack on one of the beds, noticing an open en suite bathroom door, but making a beeline for the window.

"Oh man, you scored the good room." That was Matty from behind, in the doorway. When Kevin turned to grin at him, Matty nodded towards the other bed. "Mind if I take it?"

"Sure," Kevin agreed quickly.

Chris was coming upstairs behind them. "So I get the third one, whatever it is? To myself? Yeah, fine by me."

"Oh, shit, you had that planned all along!" CJ laughed from the room down the hall.

"He's a tricky bastard," Matty snorted. He tossed his bag on the other bed, then joined Kevin by the window for a sec. "Wow, this is… gorgeous."

The few trees framing their view had green buds on

them, and at this level, they could actually see a bird's nest tucked into one of the branches, almost hidden by a flush of new growth. The lake beyond was calm, the wind still low.

"Come on, guys. Food time," CJ called out.

Matty gave Kevin one of his trademark gorgeous smiles and then turned to lead them both out of the house, down to the deck where the guys were putting together sandwiches and distributing beer cans.

Kevin tried not to watch Matty in his hot henley shirt and beige shorts as he lounged on a picnic bench, laughing at the guys' jokes and pushing his hair back and just...

Being adorable.

God, Kevin had to get it together. Even being jammed in the backseat with two guys had done nothing for him, but standing next to Matty overlooking a romantic view?

His chest was tight with excitement, and he pulled out his cell. Wow, the reception was crap out here—not even 3G. Even GPRS was struggling out here. That was fine, though. This was just a relaxing island getaway weekend... the less Facebook, the better.

Kevin took a beer from CJ and cracked it open, then busied himself helping CJ make sandwiches for them all. The rest of them dragged chairs around the picnic table and set it with placemats and pitchers of ice water.

It was easy to join in their casual banter as they ate and washed up the few dishes, then headed down to the dock with lawn chairs.

"Swimming already? Jesus!" Kevin laughed as CJ came out in board shorts. "Do you hate yourself and want to cramp up and drown?"

"That's a rumor, dude. Urban legend."

Kevin clicked his tongue. "I'm not counting on it."

"Hey, can I have your TV?" Chris joined in.

"I'll take his computer," Fisher agreed.

"Fuck off, all of you." CJ braced himself with a deep breath, then took a running jump off the edge of the deck and cannonballed into the water, sending the rest of them scattering.

Within half an hour, everyone but Kevin and Matty was in the water, and Matty sat on the edge with his legs in the water.

Instead, Kevin stretched out on a deck chair on the dock and stripped his t-shirt off to enjoy the nice sun and summer heat. Maybe he could pick up a bit of a tan.

Matty was shirtless, too.

Kevin was *not* looking over at him. Lying back with the sun in his eyes sounded preferable to getting a hard-on for Matty while in shorts with everyone else watching.

They were talking about a player he didn't know, so Kevin laced his fingers behind his head and pushed his sunglasses up his nose, then leaned back in the deck chair.

This was the good life.

⸻

The afternoon hours crawled by, and at last, Kevin figured it couldn't hurt to get a little water. He headed inside for another beer and to change into swim trunks.

He didn't bother closing the bedroom door before he stripped off his shorts and underwear to step into his swim trunks.

Of course, *then*, he heard the patio door slide open and footsteps on the stairs.

Kevin nearly tripped over his shorts and banged his shin

on the edge of his bed in his haste to yank up the trunks, since he had a horrible feeling he knew who it was.

Sure enough, he was right.

"Hey," Matty greeted, recoiling for a moment in surprise. "S-Sorry," he added in a quick, staccato laugh. "You good?"

"It's cool, bro," Kevin answered automatically.

"Enjoying it?"

"Yeah, yeah, it's good." Kevin folded his shorts and underwear and shoved them into his backpack, then went to take another look out their gorgeous bedroom window. "Great spot here."

It only took a glance down at the water to see everyone else still hanging around the edge of the dock, which meant they were definitely alone in the house. They weren't even looking at the house at all, too invested in some kind of passionate discussion which had CJ slapping the water.

"Fantastic," Matty agreed quietly, walking up beside him. Kevin finally spared him a quick look, then glanced a second time.

Water droplets still trickled down Matty's back, his shorts damp, but he'd been sitting out of the water for a couple minutes so he wasn't dripping all over the house.

Instead, he was at that gorgeous stage of water beading along his skin, his skin shining with a healthy sun-kissed glow. And he was muscled, a couple scars running along his chest and side.

"Fights?" Kevin nodded at one of them. Then, his cheeks turned hot. He'd pretty much admitted he was staring at Matty's hot body.

Matty smirked slightly and looked out the window again, then glanced up and down Kevin. "Yeah, that one was," he pointed at his side. "A skate."

"Ouch."

"The other's not from the ice." Matty stepped a little closer, his eyes catching and fixing on Kevin's now. Those beautiful eyes held a question, too.

Kevin thought it was something like *do you want this?*, but he wasn't sure. He swallowed and held his ground as Matty stepped closer, and then…

Matty's hands were on his sides. This was way more than a friendly move.

Kevin leaned in to press a quick, hot kiss against Matty's lips, his dick stirring with interest as his chest heated up instantly.

A nearly-naked, wet guy whose trunks were clinging to the outline of his dick grabbing him around the waist and pulling him in? Uh, yes, please.

More importantly, it was *Matty* pulling him in. His hands rose to run over Matty's damp shoulders.

Then, Kevin's breath caught in his throat and he darted a quick sideways glance out the window before trying to pull back again. Matty's hands were firm around his waist still, though, keeping him in place.

"D'you mind?" Kevin muttered.

"They wouldn't give a fuck, and anyway, they're not looking."

Kevin's heart pounded. He let Matty keep him in his hold —he wasn't clutching him so tightly Kevin couldn't break away anyway. He leaned in for another kiss or two before his nerves started to grind at him again.

Once again, Matty kept him close, his expression curious. His lips were still parted and moist, his eyes dark with lust as he watched Kevin.

Kevin's cheeks flushed with heat as he rubbed his neck. "Shut up."

"I didn't say anything," Matty chuckled.

Kevin kissed him once more, finally taking the time to focus on *kissing* him instead of trying to kiss him and dart away again. When he focused on Matty's face up close—those long lashes, his full lips, his smooth skin interrupted only by the rough stubble along his jaw...

God, he was *gorgeous* up close.

And Kevin wanted a lot more of this. But Kevin couldn't help but ask, "You sure you don't mind?"

"If they see, they see. Whatever," Matty murmured. "We've been drinking. We've all seen our buddies do more when they're drunk."

Kevin laughed under his breath and shrugged his agreement. "They wouldn't out us or...?"

Us. It was a weird word considering they hadn't actually talked about what the fuck this was becoming, but it seemed too early to assume it was going anywhere at all.

Matty shook his head slightly, his expression warm. "They're cool. They would never."

Just having Matty's word that they were cool was enough to set Kevin's nerves at ease. He nodded, stepping closer to Matty and away from the window to face him properly and slide his arms around his waist.

They were touching more now, Matty's thigh sliding between Kevin's as their bare legs rubbed, their stomachs touching... Then, Matty's damp chest pressed against Kevin's, and Kevin was certain Matty could feel the way his heart pounded with arousal as he leaned in to press their lips together in a hot, wet slide of lips on lips, tongues clashing again and teeth clicking with how hard they both went in for the kiss.

His whole body was tight with *wanting*, and he was gonna need to jump right into cold water now, but he gave in to the impulse to run his hand up that strong back and over his shoulders, then up the back of his neck to tangle in that thick, soft-looking hair.

God, Matty's hair felt amazing to run his hands through, but better yet were the hot lips against his own and the way Matty was softly panting into his mouth, moaning in the back of the throat every time Kevin ground their hips together, both their cocks half-hard now.

"Okay, we gotta..." Kevin laughed breathlessly, pulling away from Matty and trying desperately to catch his breath. If he didn't stop now, he was gonna need a lot more than making out.

Matty laughed breathlessly, too, and raised a hand to run through his hair, unintentionally giving Kevin a flash of that strong bicep behind his head. For half a second, he looked like he belonged in a magazine.

No, it was too late to just jump in the lake. Kevin was gonna need the bathroom.

"I'll head down," Matty offered, even though his eyes were raking up and down Kevin's body before fixing on his face again.

It was unspoken: wait a couple minutes before coming out. Don't be too suspicious. Even if Matty didn't care if his buddies found out, neither of them wanted to answer *those* questions.

Kevin jerked his chin in a quick nod. "Yeah. Cool, man." He turned tail to flee for the bathroom. Waiting a couple minutes wasn't gonna be a problem. It'd take a couple minutes to jerk off anyway to the fresh body memory of Matty's strong hands on his hips, the flat ripples of his stomach against his, the knee between his legs, the half-hard cock rubbing against his own through their swim trunks…

Now that he'd had a taste of Matty—and such a fucking *good* one—he wasn't sure he could control himself around him for a whole weekend.

CHAPTER
Seventeen

MATTY

Fisher was gutting fish.

It was all Matty could do to resist the pun, but from the way Fisher kept eyeing him every time he flicked his knife along a fish's spine, he knew exactly what he was thinking.

"Sorry!" Matty laughed. It wasn't just the name pun bugging him, to be fair. Fisher was also taking his sweet time —Matty could do it faster. He'd gone fishing a lot around home a lot.

"Oh, is Fisher not done gutting fish yet? Jesus, for your namesake you're fuckin' slow," CJ called from the back deck.

Fisher groaned, but he joined in laughing with Matty and CJ. "I've *never* heard that before. Congratulations. Brand new idea," he called out.

A minute later, he had the last few fish pieces ready to slide onto the plate. "All done?" Matty asked.

"Yep. Go bring 'em to that asshole."

Matty snorted with laughter and brought the plate up to the grill on the deck. "Here you are, asshole," he cheerfully told CJ. "Your boyfriend sent these."

CJ fluttered his lashes. "How romantic!" He threw them on the grill, brushing them swiftly with oil while Matty went to check on Kevin and Chris. There were already sausages, potatoes, and corn loaded onto the grill, so there wasn't a lot of prep left to do.

Chris was kicking back at the picnic table while Kevin tossed a salad. All day, he'd been trying to make himself useful—from carrying coolers to making sandwiches for lunch and bringing more drinks down to the dock for them all.

Matty was dying to pull him aside and tell him he didn't have to try so hard, but he hadn't really had a chance to get him alone since that kiss not long after lunch.

After that, he and Fisher had gone to the other dock—the old one, on the other side of the little island—to catch these fish for supper while the others stayed on the newer one so they didn't stomp around and disturb the fish. And then it had taken a while to get supper ready, and… they just hadn't had a moment yet.

Not like that moment earlier. Jesus Christ, that was hot, and he couldn't let himself think about rubbing up against that gorgeous body for more than three seconds at a time.

That was the end of *this* three seconds, so he distracted himself by calling out, "How long 'till everything's done?"

"Maybe five minutes?"

"Oh, jeez. Almost there then. Okay."

"Good," Kevin spoke up, scooping the salad bowl under his arm to carry out to the back deck. "This is done, too."

"That's it for inside, then." Matty shut the door on the way out to keep the slightly cooler inside air in, then helped serve up supper.

They talked about random shit over supper as always, but

Matty kept sneaking glances at Kevin. He seemed relaxed enough, despite how skittish he'd acted earlier when he'd thought everyone would stare up and through the trees at their bedroom window while they were kissing.

It was a given that Kevin was partly closeted, but it seemed like maybe he cared even more than Matty about maintaining that, despite playing at a lower level. Matty just hoped Kevin's helpfulness wasn't from being worried he didn't fit in or that they wouldn't like him if they found out their secret.

After supper, Matty stuck around to do the dishes while everyone stayed up late talking in the living room. Tired though he was, he determinedly stuck it out as, one by one, the other three guys crashed and headed to bed to sleep off their big, late supper and busy day of relaxation.

That left just the two of them, at fucking *last*, to talk and… well… do whatever.

Matty's heart jolted as he nodded down to the dock. "Wanna head out for a bit?"

"Ready to fend off the black flies?" Kevin countered with a laugh. At night, they wouldn't be nearly as bad as they were at dusk, but still…

"I got a citronella belt clip thing." Matty patted it. "We're good within fifteen feet."

"Jesus, that's smart. I want one," Kevin grinned. "I guess I'll stay closer than fifteen feet."

I want you a lot closer than that.

Matty swallowed and grabbed his t-shirt, shrugging it on before he pulled open the patio door. "Aprés-vous."

"Ohhh, the formal. What'd I do wrong?" Kevin laughed.

"You remember high school French?"

"Who fuckin' doesn't," Kevin groaned rhetorically, sliding the door shut after them.

They wandered down the steps to the dock where they'd spent most of the day. It was quiet now aside from the incessant backdrop of crickets and frogs along the banks. It was a constant, high-pitched song, but Kevin associated it with things like this—camping with buddies and quiet fireside conversations.

"We gonna do a bonfire tomorrow?"

"Fuck, yeah," Matty answered. "There's a fire pit down the other side of the island there."

"Perfect." Kevin dropped into a chair and stretched out, wiggling his toes.

Matty smiled as the movement caught his eye, then dragged the deck chair right next to Kevin's and sat in it.

"Stars are already coming out."

Matty leaned back for a look, letting his eyes adjust to the darkness. "So they are." There weren't a lot yet, a slight hazy layer of clouds obscuring part of the sky, but that seemed to be blowing off as it darkened. He could see a couple constellations, at least. "Pretty out here."

"It is," Kevin murmured. "Don't often get to do this."

"Not during the summers?"

"Nah. I was usually in town working, to pay for tuition or whatever," Kevin laughed. "Or pay for camps, gear... you know how it goes."

"Yeah," Matty murmured. "It's not easy. I worked a part-time job during school too, 'till I came here."

"What year did you leave?"

"Second year."

Kevin whistled under his breath.

Matty laughed quietly. "Not 'cause I'm awesome or anything. They were just desperate."

"I dunno about that, man. Your Wikipedia page says otherwise."

This caught Matty off-guard, and he laughed a short, sharp sound that made Kevin flinch with surprise. "You Googled me?"

"Fuck yeah, I Googled your ass before I came to a deserted island with you."

Matty snorted. "What'd you find?"

"Not as many gay rumors as I thought."

That made Matty smirk, at least. So they were slowly coming around to the subject—but neither of them seemed to want to bring it up yet. "Everyone's pretty careful not to point a finger until there's proof."

"Mmm." Kevin gazed off across the water, and Matty stole the moment to look at him—the moonlight framing those sharp cheekbones and his firm jaw.

God, he was so damn beautiful. Matty hoped he didn't wreck his face playing this fucking sport.

Then, Matty wondered if he was thinking of someone. Had he had boyfriends before? How quiet would they stay if and when Kevin got big?

"It's rough, not getting these moments a lot," Matty offered to give him the chance to talk. "Especially not having a lot of buddies outside the game."

"Yeah. You get a whole new family inside it, but you lose everyone outside," Kevin agreed with a quiet chuckle. "I'm lucky I've got a second family, pretty much... Cam's buddies... but other than that, not a lot of friends anymore."

Matty nodded. "And as you move up, it's that slow cull of

everyone from the towns around you until you're the only guy you know from your city, huh?" He was the only one he knew from Timmins around his age, though there were some older and one or two younger guys, too. And aside from Cam and now Kevin, he couldn't think of anyone else from Fredericton.

Not that that mattered too much—once you were on a team with a guy, you could become almost kin with him by the end of a season.

"Really sucks when they're gone because you kicked their ass," Kevin murmured.

Matty was startled into another little laugh. "Yeah. I know, though." It sounded egotistic, but when you were one of the better players in the draft... well, it set up tensions.

"God, it's just a life of its own," Kevin murmured, then finally glanced at him. "But it's worth it so far. How are you finding it?"

Matty leaned forward a little and braced his elbows. "It's good. It's... it's a lot like you're used to, but *more*. Just more intense, a lot more media and fan attention, more pressure, more violent on the body..."

Kevin nodded silently.

"This time next year you'll be in just as rough shape as I was this summer. Hopefully even worse-off if you get to the finals," Matty grinned. "But yeah. Finding someone who understands that is... hard."

It was a silent, tentative gesture, and Matty could see how fucking nervous it made Kevin: he put out his hand to rest on the arm of Matty's chair.

How goddamn sweet.

Instantly, Matty covered Kevin's hand with his own, running his thumb down Kevin's.

And almost instantly, his brain went into overdrive: why

the hell should he get close to this guy when he might not even be around that long? He could get traded to another team, he could lose his spot before the season even began, he could get sick, and then that would be long-distance hell.

But he took a deep breath, then slid his hand under Kevin's.

And I don't even know him, not really, even though I Googled him probably just as much as he Googled me...

Matty let his shoulders sink and the tension drain from his body again when Kevin didn't pull back. He had to give this a shot.

Their fingers tangled, their eyes locked, it was hard to say who made the first move. Both of them leaned across the arms of their chairs, their hands now firmly gripping each other's as they twisted sideways to make the connection.

Lips met lips. Matty was getting to know how Kevin tasted, and even better, how he kissed.

Kevin's kisses were slow at first, tentative, like he wasn't quite sure that he was welcome. Once Matty had been kissing him back for a few seconds, his kisses were deep and sensual, his lips moving with precision along Matty's to suck or nip at just the right spots.

Matty burned with heat, his fingers running along Kevin's, but Kevin squeezed his hand tighter.

They broke apart to gasp for breath, both laughing under their breath even though nothing was that funny.

Matty just felt a *glow* in his chest that he didn't know how else to express. And his dick, but he knew exactly how to handle *that*... preferably roughly.

The mental image of his swim trunks hauled down, Kevin pressed up behind him with one strong arm around his waist like earlier, his other hand jerking his hand up and down

Matty's shaft as he pressed those beautiful pink lips against the soft spots behind Matty's ear…

Fuck. Fuck, fuck, *fuck*, he wanted that so bad he almost couldn't breathe.

"Yeah," Kevin breathed out, his voice hoarse for a second and eyes hazy. Christ, were his thoughts as dirty as Matty's right now? Then, he cleared his throat. "Yeah, we probably shouldn't…"

"Make a habit of this? Kissing in public?" Matty grinned.

"Have we ever *not* kissed in public?" Kevin laughed, and Matty joined in. They dropped hands as they rose to their feet, pushing back their deck chairs.

Then, Matty's smile faded slightly as he watched Kevin's expression. *Do you want to?*

But he didn't dare ask it yet.

He wasn't sure he'd earned the right to.

"I'm heading in to bed," Kevin murmured after a second, finally blinking and glancing away at the stars again. "Staying out?"

"For a minute," Matty nodded, his chest tightening. No way could he jack off with his buddies right there inside, but maybe he'd jump in the water for a late-night swim if this burn in his stomach didn't fade. "Be there soon. I'll try not to wake you up."

"Okay. See you."

Matty waited until the purr of the patio door shutting faded, then glanced out over the water once more and let out a long, slow breath.

Something was going on, and every time he tried to screw up his courage to address it, he found himself with one thought on his mind: maybe Kevin just didn't want to label it. Worse yet, maybe he was so closeted he didn't want to think about it. Pushing him too hard now might mean they never found out how good they could be together.

They'd only met a couple weeks ago, for fuck's sakes. It wasn't like they'd been playing this game for years, but even days felt like too long to wait now that Matty had had a taste of him.

This weekend, he promised himself. *Even if I have to talk to him on the fucking boat on the way back. I'll find a way.*

When his boner had subsided enough that he knew he wasn't gonna make a pass at Kevin, Matty hauled himself to his feet to head in and get some sleep.

CHAPTER
Eighteen
KEVIN

THE SMELL OF BACON TICKLED KEVIN'S NOSE. HE STRETCHED slowly, rubbing his face against cool-smelling sheets. That was weird. That was definitely not his usual laundry soap.

Oh, *yeah*.

He cracked his eyes, shielding his eyes against the light spilling in between the wood slats of the blinds. The wall of windows was too bright for ordinary blinds to hold back the morning sun on a day as gorgeous as this one had to be.

Then, his chest jolted. He jerked his head around so fast he nearly strained his neck, glancing over at the other single bed.

Matty was asleep on his front, the covers mostly pulled over him, but one arm was stretched out above the pillow.

Kevin swallowed hard, dragging his gaze off the way the covers rippled around his body before he could start to imagine what was under which ripples in the blankets.

Instead, he hauled the covers off himself and grabbed a fresh change of clothes, then let himself into the en suite bathroom to get ready for the morning. At least with all the time they were spending in the water, he didn't feel like he had to shower, and neither had he brought his razor. He'd deal with being a little bristly today.

Matty still wasn't up by the time he left the en suite, so he headed straight downstairs to the kitchen.

"Morning," Chris greeted. He looked like the only one up so far. "Sleep well?"

"Yeah, like a rock. You?"

"Same," Chris told him as he approached the fridge. "I'm doing bacon and potatoes, eggs, sausages, uh…"

"Toast? I can do toast," Kevin laughed. "Are they almost up?"

"Oh, yeah. Good one. Yeah, I'll dump cold water on them if they're not up within a couple more minutes. I heard a lot of angry grunting from CJ and Fisher's room, though."

As he loaded the toaster with bread, Kevin chuckled. "So, you been out here before?"

"Oh, no. I've only been living here a couple years. Last summer I spent pretty much the whole thing with my family."

"Where you from?" Kevin hopped onto the counter and sat there, swinging his feet now and then. Chris had an American accent, but he couldn't tell what kind.

"Nevada."

"No shit. That's a long way away."

Chris chuckled. "Yeah, I know. Got traded up here, and… I dunno, I kinda like it. All the snow's a nice change."

"From the desert? I think we'd all trade you," Kevin laughed.

Chris chuckled. "Yeah. You're from Fredericton like Cam, right?"

"You were all good buddies with him, weren't you?"

Kevin asked, kicking the drawers lightly with heels before he hooked his toes in the drawer handle. "Everyone won't stop asking me about him."

"Sorry," Chris laughed. "Yeah, he's a real good guy. Not all guys leave that kind of impression on you."

Briefly, Kevin wondered: had Cam dated any of these guys? Had he dated Matty? That would be weird. But he pushed aside the thought and half-smiled. "Yeah, he is. He warned me about Coach Walker."

"He'll be a hard-ass, but only 'cause he wants to see you get better."

Kevin nodded. "I appreciate that."

There were footsteps on the stairs, and Matty appeared a moment later in almost identical beige shorts to yesterday's outfit and a white shirt with faded pink and orange stripes. With flip-flops and a fishing rod, he'd look like an obnoxious straight frat guy, not the guy making Kevin's fingers tingle with the memory of his.

Matty had nice, strong hands.

Fucking hell, I'm gay.

"Morning," Kevin said, feeling like he'd been staring for minutes even if all of that had flashed through his head in seconds.

"Hey," Matty greeted. "Breakfast almost done? Need me to go scare up CJ and Fisher?"

"Nope," CJ hollered. "Be right there."

Matty frowned in disappointment. "Fine, I won't." He jumped down the last three stairs, then swung around the bannister and strode over to grab himself a plate. He had a few moments of not really looking at Kevin, but once he glanced his way a couple times, that passed.

Realizing he'd been watching Matty a little too long,

Kevin tore his eyes off him and went to do the same. By the time they'd served up their own breakfasts, the other guys were downstairs and following suit.

Kevin only noticed how relaxed he was at the end of breakfast. He was joining in conversations more now, and it felt like they welcomed him as a buddy, not just Matty's friend.

After breakfast, they headed down to set up their fishing rods by the lake. Kevin wasn't that interested in fishing himself, but he was fine watching the others. They all scattered across the island—CJ and Fisher on the old dock, Chris on the new dock, and Matty on the shoreline.

Kevin joined Chris first, shooting the shit. He wound up staying for an hour or two before heading over to join Matty, folding lawn chair under his arm.

Once he had it unfolded and plopped next to Matty's, he leaned back and stretched. "How's the fishing?" He leaned over and looked in the bucket—nothing so far.

"Slow today," Matty shrugged and yawned. "No big."

"Cool."

Matty was sprawled across his chair, his legs out at odd angles, his arm stretched over the arm of the chair, hand on the top of the tackle box.

Kevin drew a slow breath, then reached out to cover Matty's hand with his own for a few moments. When Kevin glanced at Matty, Matty's eyes flickered to him. He gave him a slow, quiet smile that just about melted Kevin's heart.

"All right?" Matty asked simply.

"Yeah," Kevin hummed and closed his eyes for a few moments. This was the most affection he dared initiate in public, but Matty turned his hand over so their palms nestled together and that was enough for him.

More than enough.

***

"Ohhh, look at my muscles, bro."

"My biceps are bigger than yours."

"I do a hundred one-handed pushups every morning."

Kevin couldn't breathe from laughing at the mocking Matty was enduring from his buddies. All he'd done was announce that he was doing his daily workout in the house for the next bit, if anyone wanted to join him.

Everyone else was in the water, splashing and shaming him, except Kevin, who stretched out on the dock with his feet on the water and laughed until his stomach hurt.

"What did I ever do wrong?" Matty lamented, trying to grab the edge of the dock to haul himself up.

"Where do we start?" CJ tried to hook his finger in Matty's waistband.

Matty slapped his hand away and laughed. "Fuck off, all of you. If you wanna work out, I'll be in the house. Training season doesn't stop just 'cause it's sunny today."

"I'll come," Kevin offered and pushed himself up from the dock. Finally, maybe they could… talk about some of this. Like the fact that Matty's eyes kept glazing over every time he looked at Kevin in his swim trunks.

The two men wandered up the short flight of stairs to the back deck, walking slowly to let themselves dry off before they got to the house.

"How's it going, then?" Matty casually asked Kevin. "Liking it out here?"

"Yeah, it's pretty sweet. Everyone seems friendly."

Matty smiled. "Yeah, they like you. I knew they would."

"Cool," Kevin laughed, giving Matty a quick smile of relief. "Always weird being the new guy."

"Yeah. That's why I wanted you to come along this week-end," Matty nodded. "They'll keep an eye out for you." He pulled open the patio door to let them both inside.

At the same moment, they breathed sighs of relief and enjoyment. The air conditioning wasn't great here, but it was still less humid than baking on the dock, plus a few degrees colder.

Matty was still damp from the water, and he started to shiver almost right away.

"Nippy?" Kevin teased.

"Yeah." Matty rubbed his arms and chest.

Kevin laughed and reached out to tweak one of Matty's nipples. They were hard as diamonds. When he rubbed it, it only softened slightly under his touch.

Matty laughed, turning to face Kevin and step towards him. He ran his hand up along Kevin's side, his eyes catching Kevin's. In a heartbeat, it had gone from two friends being buddies to…

To whatever this was.

"Nipple," Kevin murmured, then flicked the nipple with a fingertip.

Matty couldn't stop the gasp that parted his lips and made his eyes go a little hazy as he tipped his chin up.

Oooh, he was sensitive, was he? Kevin was going to enjoy this.

Kevin cast a quick glance out to the patio, but nobody was even in sight nearby. Through the slats of the porch rail-ings, he could faintly see the outlines of the other guys bobbing around the water still.

Reassured and emboldened, he stepped close enough and

leaned to press a kiss over one of those hard nipples, rolling the other between his fingers while he gripped Matty's hip tightly.

"Hnnh," Matty sighed, his nails digging into Kevin's back. "Oh, fuck."

"That warm you up a little?" Kevin murmured, his hot breath ghosting across Matty's nipple.

Matty laughed breathlessly and nodded. "Fuck, yeah. Jesus, let me work out first, or I'll…" he trailed off.

"Be tempted to skip your workout?" Kevin teased, letting go of Matty and stepping back again with just a brush of his lips across Matty's shoulder. "Okay. Tell me what we're doing."

He loved that it took Matty a few seconds to focus his eyes again and adjust his swim trunks. "R-Right. Pushups." Matty dropped to his stomach on the floor, bracing himself on his toes.

Kevin smirked and followed suit, mirroring Matty as he moved through the usual routine. Watching Matty's muscles flex from head to toe as he worked on his biceps, triceps, abs, and core strength was pretty much Kevin's idea of a perfect afternoon.

And holding his feet down while he did those crunches? Kevin smirked at the memory of their stolen kisses in the gym, watching Matty's cheeks flushing steadily more red with exertion.

Once that was done, it was on to the final plank, and he stretched out alongside Matty, tensing up his whole body. That wasn't hard; his muscles naturally wanted to tighten with arousal.

He curled his fingers into his palms so hard the nails bit into his skin. Maybe Matty didn't want to hook up in a lake house with his buddies just down at the end of the dock.

It was really fucking hard to focus on that when the rasp of Matty's rough breathing kept digging into his self-control, chipping away at the flimsy restraint.

Especially when Matty breathed out, "Three, two, one… done," melted against the floor, and turned that dark gaze on him.

Kevin nearly lost his breath as he met Matty's gaze, rolling slowly onto his side before sitting up. His muscles ached, but that faded as fast as blinking when his cock demanded attention again.

Matty was just so close…

And Matty was thinking along the same lines. His eyes were down on Kevin's groin now, following the outline of his cock against the loose swim trunks. Considerably less loose now than they had been a minute ago.

"We should go upstairs," Matty murmured after a few long moments, and by the tone of his voice, Kevin knew he wasn't just suggesting they change into fresh shorts.

Kevin rocked up and onto his feet, grabbing Matty's upper arm to haul him up to his feet. He was a solid weight, but he was scrambling up just as fast as Kevin could yank him up.

And they were kissing again, walking towards the stairs all tangled in each other. Their hands were on each other's chests and hips, cocks hard and pressing into one another through the scarce few layers of fabric. Their bodies were hot, sweaty and rubbing against one another's, nipples brushing nipples for sharp, unexpected bursts of sensation through Kevin's chest.

Matty sucked on Kevin's neck, just below his ear, until

Kevin's knees just about buckled and he grabbed the railing of the staircase hard. "Oh, *fuck*." Matty's stubble scraped his neck, and he almost couldn't think.

Matty chuckled deeply, then slapped Kevin's ass to get him upstairs first. Predictably, he could only wait a step or two before those broad hands were on Kevin's ass, squeezing and kneading.

"Nnh," Kevin moaned his approval, rounding the top of the stairs and slamming his way into the bedroom.

Matty shoved the door shut with Kevin's body, pinning him up against it like he was boarding him.

Luckily, Kevin was expecting it. He grunted as he hit the door, grabbing Matty's hips to haul him in close.

Their lips met roughly at first in quick, hard, open-mouthed kisses. They had to get that out of the way first— the raw desire for skin on skin, wet lips catching and biting, noses rubbing, hands squeezing and pulling until the weight of Matty up against him made it hard to breathe.

With Matty sucking the tip of his tongue, it was really fucking hard to focus on what he wanted to do to him, but Matty had his own ideas. After a couple seconds, he let go of Kevin's shoulder and ran his hand down Kevin's chest, igniting a quick burn everywhere his fingertips trailed. He was halfway down Kevin's stomach when Kevin realized where this was going and moaned a loud, sharp approval.

Matty laughed against Kevin's mouth, then licked his way in again. Kevin nearly lost his footing at the hot, wet tongue against his own, sliding between his lips, and the hand suddenly shoving its way down his trunks and past the clingy mesh netting to wrap around his shaft and jerk it a couple times.

"Nnnh!" Kevin whimpered, jerking his hips forward into that hand.

Matty pulled away from his kisses, leaving him gasping for breath, and sank to his knees.

"Oh, Jesus fucking Christ."

Kevin was going to come in ten seconds flat at this rate. He was already throbbing with heat as Matty hauled down his shorts, exposing his raging boner to the open air.

Matty smirked, looking him up and down slowly from where he knelt between Kevin's legs. He ran his tongue along his bottom lip. "Been waiting for this view."

Kevin's thighs clenched and trembled as he struggled to think of a smart-ass reply. All he managed was, "You look good there."

Matty winked, that devilish smile back on his face for a second. "Not to kill the moment, but you get tested and shit?"

"Yeah, man," Kevin breathed out. "I'm clean."

"Negative for everything?"

Kevin didn't miss the reproach in Matty's tone, and he winced. "Yeah. Sorry. You?"

As fast as that, Matty was over it and winking at him. "Me, too. You cool if I just…" He wrapped his hand around Kevin's cock again, slowly jerking it and bringing the tip close to his lips.

"Fucking go to town," Kevin growled under his breath, cupping Matty's cheek and pushing his hair back with his thumb.

Matty wrapped those full lips around his cock head, the wet warmth barely sinking in before Matt's lips were sliding down his shaft to the base.

Ohhhh, yeah, Kevin thought so loudly he wasn't sure if

he'd also moaned it out loud. He gritted his teeth and grunted his pleasure when Matty rubbed a tight fist up and down the base, focusing his sucking on the sensitive head and first couple inches.

It was like Matty already knew exactly what he wanted, and all he had to do was lean back, somehow stay on his feet, and enjoy it.

"Yes," Kevin panted when Matty's tongue tickled at his slit and swiped under the head, then around it. A few licks later, Matty was back to sucking his cheeks in around his shaft and pushing his lips down.

The heat and pressure were goddamn perfect, and Kevin's body was already tightening. Just looking at Matty's hair spilling into his eyes, his stubbly cheeks pulled in around his shaft, the thick lips sliding around reddened, stiff flesh… it all had him on edge. Every time Matty's eyes flickered up his body to meet his eyes, Kevin curled his toes into the floor.

"Yes, Matt—Matty, I'm gonna…" he warned in a breathy pant, but Matty just pushed his head further down, that sensitive spot on his shaft sliding over the back of his tongue, and he was coming…!

Kevin smacked the back of his head against the door as his hips shoved forward in quick, hard thrusts with each clench and shudder of his muscles.

"Yes…! Matty!"

Matty gave one short, sharp moan, and his tongue worked under and around Kevin's cock as he swallowed, his eyes fixed up on Kevin's face, like…

Like he couldn't stop watching Kevin.

Kevin blushed hard, all the blood now rushing from his cock straight to his face. He almost couldn't look Matty in the eye, but he didn't want to miss a second of himself sliding over Matty's lips as Matty knelt back and wiped his mouth.

"Fuckin' *hot*," Matty breathed out reverently. It was impossible to miss the tent poking up from his own shorts.

Kevin smirked and grabbed Matty's shoulder to, once again, haul him to his feet. This time, he pushed him to the bed, ignoring the slight ache in his back from being thrown into the door. When Matty sat on the edge, Kevin dropped to his knees between his legs, already pressing kisses up his inner thighs.

"Oh my God, dude," Matty breathed out. "Fuck, I'm already really... really hot."

"You liked sucking me off that much?" Kevin teased, yanking open the strings on the front of his shorts. He pulled them down to Matty's thighs.

Matty's cock was finally freed, standing stiffly up in the air and just begging for his attention. Aside from furtive shower glances, Kevin hadn't had the chance to really see it, let alone in all its glory.

"Tasty," Kevin teased, leaning in to drag his tongue from the very base to the tip as he wrapped his hand around the throbbing shaft.

Matty's response was a short, stifled whimper in the back of his throat, and he raised his hand to bite the side of his fist. It was an almost shy look, and it absolutely captivated Kevin.

Kevin loved the salty musk against his tongue. It had been months since he'd tasted a guy, but now that he had his mouth wrapped around a hot, hard dick, he could suddenly remember why he loved giving head so much. Every little lick of his tongue or extra sucking-in of his cheeks made Matty twitch or tremble, his muscles tense up...

He listened to Matty's breath catching and the quiet grunts spilling from his lips, and the nails digging into his shoulder told him when he was going just fast enough up and down the shaft, Matty's pleasure in the palm of his hand —and in his mouth.

Just before he could really get into the spirit, Matty shoved his shoulder, his breath catching as he mumbled, "I'm gonna—dude, if you don't wanna swallow, now's your chance…"

But fuck, no. Matty tasted amazing, with just a hint of sweaty saltiness, and he wanted to see how *all* of him tasted.

He kept his hand on Matty's stomach when he came so that he didn't grind too hard into his face, but he let him fuck his mouth a little. The way Matty's eyes widened, red staining his cheeks, it had been a while since he'd gotten to do this, too.

"Oh my God, that was… fuckin' fantastic."

Kevin slowly drew his mouth off Matty's cock and leaned back on his heels to swallow, giving him a broad grin. "Mmm, yeah. You taste great." Slightly sweet, slightly salty, kinda pleasant, really.

He didn't expect Matty to blush even harder at that than he had at the sight of Kevin on his knees in the first place. God, Matty was adorable.

When Kevin rose, it was Matty's turn to help haul him back to his feet. "Wanna brush your teeth?" Matty offered, his eyes sparkling.

"Suppose so," Kevin smirked. "Like that won't be suspicious as fuck. Both of us with minty-fresh breath…"

"Well, don't use my toothpaste, then." Matty snorted.

"Stop me." Kevin swiped a taste of Matty's weird ultra-whitening toothpaste before Matty could grab the tube, then put his thumb to his mouth to suck it off. "Ew." It was like being slapped in the face with a whole mint bush. "I'll stick with my own, thanks," he concluded and squeezed some out onto his toothbrush.

Matty was pressed up against his side as he brushed his teeth, trying to muscle him out of the way of the sink, but Kevin stood his ground until it was time to rinse and spit. When Matty was leaning down under the flow of water for one last rinse, Kevin shoved his head down under it for a moment, then laughed and fled to the bedroom.

Matty caught up with him in two seconds flat, his mouth still wet and minty, grabbing Kevin by the back of his swim shorts and hauling him back to kiss him obnoxiously.

Once the initial punishment was over, Kevin took advantage of the moment to press a few more slow kisses against Matty's lips, tangling his hand in the back of Matty's hair. They had to be making out for a good minute before Kevin realized he was losing track of time pressed up against Matty's body, their arms around each other. He laughed as he pulled away, and so did Matty.

"Last one in the lake has to give a freebie." With that, Matty was off like a shot and Kevin was hot on his heels.

Not that Kevin *minded* giving Matty a free blowjob... pretty much anytime, anywhere.

They furiously pounded down the stairs, out to the deck, and down to the dock. Kevin held his breath for the cannon-ball moment, fighting his way around Matty trying to block his way to the water.

It was hard to say who hit the water first, but everyone was laughing nonetheless.

CHAPTER
Nineteen

MATTY

"You just got back today? Dude, you both look trashed."

Matty swapped looks with CJ and scoffed. "Thanks, man," he laughed at Fleet. "You look like shit yourself."

Fleet had an excuse, though—he was coming down from a Saturday night hangover with a little hair of the dog this Sunday evening. Matty's only excuse was packing up and taking the drive back from the cabin, and even that had flown by with such good company.

"You gonna be sober enough for your medical tomorrow?" Matty added, jerking his thumb at Fleet's pint glass.

Fleet laughed. "I'm taking it easy, man. So, what's up with bringing Kevin along?"

Matty frowned in confusion and tilted his head. What did Fleet mean? It wasn't like anyone around here hated him. "Huh?"

"I mean, apparently he's got someone back in New Brunswick..." Fleet scooted his stool closer to CJ and Matty and leaned in, keeping his voice low. "A guy."

Matty quirked a brow. For his sake, he really fucking hoped that wasn't true, but the gist of it could well be.

"He really gay, you think?" Fleet asked them.

CJ shrugged and looked at Matty. "I dunno, man. I didn't hear him talk about New Brunswick much."

"Yeah," Matty shook his head. "I don't know if he is, but that's a pretty big rumor to spread."

"Oh, I'm not trying to be mean," Fleet instantly assured them, raising his hands.

Matty's heart clenched with worry nonetheless. "Are people talking about him?" Fleet might not mean ill, but others could. Kevin was big, but he wasn't an enforcer. Someone could do him a lot of damage—accidentally or on purpose—if word got out. He'd be a liability on the team, and that was the last thing any new guy wanted to be.

"A couple," Fleet murmured, his voice even lower now. "I'm not spreading the gossip around or anything, but you know."

"It's probably bullshit," CJ dismissed with a wave of his hand. "We go through this every year after the draft. All the rumors, and they're never true. And nobody ends up caring anyway. I mean, this is Canada."

He was originally American, even if he had dual citizenship now. He had a couple odd beliefs about Canada—including that it was somehow magically more tolerant of the gays, especially getting all up in their sports.

Yeah, *most* guys knew better than to openly bash the gay hockey player. Didn't mean some didn't want to know better. And outside sports, people were often homophobic, too—they were just too polite to say it to their faces. Even closeted, Matty had figured that shit out awfully fast. Probably because he heard a lot of from his buddies who assumed he was straight, but wouldn't have said half that shit to a gay guy if they'd known.

Matty bit back his sarcastic comment and just took another sip.

Fleet chuckled. "Yeah. But if it's true, hypothetically…"

Okay, that was enough. Matty set down his glass of Coke a little too sharply. "It's not good to gossip about shit like that," he told Fleet. "If it winds up being true, it'd have serious consequences on him. And if it's not, it would anyway."

Don't be obvious, though. Shit. The weirdness of talking about Kevin being gay, desperately hoping they didn't see the personal stake he had in it—both himself, and in his relationship with Kevin…

"Yeah," CJ chimed in, and even Fleet nodded, which made Matty relax slightly.

"Yeah, I was just wondering. I'm buddies with Jack," Fleet explained. Jack was one of their bigger guys on the minor league team—almost two-fifty even on his bad days, and built like a brick outhouse. They called him a moose some days, because when he charged someone, he was just as dangerous.

For a moment, Matty was confused. Did he think Kevin was in danger from Jack? Enforcer or not, Matty would fuck him up…

"If it does wind up being true, we'll protect him," Fleet added simply and clapped Matty's arm. "Don't worry about him."

That eased the tension a little, and Matty blinked, then sat back. "Oh. Yeah."

"Don't worry, man. For Cam's sake, if nothing else," CJ added. "He'd come punch us all if we didn't."

Matty laughed. "Yeah, he would. Yeah, we'll keep an eye on him. If the rumors get nasty… doesn't matter if they're true or not, the other guys will act like it is."

"But in *our* locker room, he'll be all right," Fleet added firmly. "It hasn't changed that much since I got called up, I'm positive."

CJ shook his head. "It definitely hasn't."

Deep in his chest, Matty was glowing. His buddies were all right, and so were the other guys.

"Whoever the first guy to come out is—major or minor leagues—in our city, he's gonna be safe," Fleet added firmly. It was a hypothetical conversation they had about once or twice a year, but year after year, nobody did. That wasn't to say nobody *was* gay… They definitely were.

They just didn't talk about it.

For Kevin's sake and his own, Matty hoped that Fleet's faith in their team was well-placed. If they kept going at the rate they already were, he couldn't see them staying secret forever.

And he didn't want to be, either.

CHAPTER
Twenty

KEVIN

ROCKING ONTO HIS BACK BLADE, CROSS OVER, AND AROUND the net.

Then... *go.*

Kevin bolted down the ice towards the net, neck and neck against Fisher. His focus didn't even break when he swerved around the stupid plastic pylons, swaying his way out of them easily and reaching the net in a spray of ice just seconds before Fisher did.

"Good!"

That was all Coach Walker had to say right now, his attention already on the next pair taking off down the ice.

Kevin swooped around and clapped Fisher's arm on the way back to the box, swinging his legs over the side and hanging out there to stay out of the way of the pairs of guys who had yet to go.

Hans was sitting by himself near the end of the bench, his skating partner not even chatting to him.

That was the weird thing—nobody seemed to be talking a lot to Hans today. Even though their main focus today was on training, most of the guys found moments to chat to each other, catch up on how their summer was going, and so on. Nobody was talking much to Hans, and when he talked to them, they only chatted for a moment before turning their attention back to someone or something else.

Kevin felt a little bad for him. Skates digging into the boards underneath, he made his way over to Hans and clapped his shoulder. "How's it going? Ready?"

"Ready," Hans agreed, giving him a quick flash of a smile before he looked at the ice again.

Kevin wasn't sure he was—after all, he hadn't really been training himself. A small part of him hoped Hans realized now why he'd been such a goddamn gym nerd all spring, but he wasn't that mean. He didn't want Hans to do badly, even if he'd been lazy.

Whatever was going on with Hans, it was kinda a weird place to have drama—the middle of their training camp.

Most of the guys were called out for another round of speed skating… this time, timed.

Fisher was captain this year, and he was handling the responsibility well—he didn't seem like a captain most of the time, except when he had to be. "Over this way," Fisher instructed the guys coming off the ice after their second round. Some were sent to the other ice, and others to the locker room.

When Kevin tried to keep Hans company on his way to the locker room, Fisher reached out to grab his arm and pull him aside for a moment. "We're going again at the end," he told him. "Wait here with me. Go on, Hans."

"Oh, cool. Okay."

The ice slowly thinned on their side as the guys gathered on the other rink instead, starting to practice stick drills.

When their side of the arena was empty except for Coach Walker and one of his assistants who was taking times, the other coaches and trainers having moved over to that ice, Fisher nodded. "Now, let's go."

Kevin stepped back onto the ice and accompanied Fisher to the end, then shook everything out and bent over in preparation for the drill.

It only took a minute at most, including getting ready. It was a good, clean drill—not a hell of a lot of footwork. Not like those goddamn crossover pylons they had to swing their feet around.

Coach Walker nodded his approval when he had what he needed and started heading to the next rink over as Fisher and Kevin stepped off the ice. "Kevin, go get a red jersey."

Kevin nodded sharply. His cheeks stung a little from the cool of the arena air, but he loved it. Finally seeing the difference even a little gym time made over a couple months was incredible. He was faster, more flexible, and a little stronger. Not hugely, but enough that he noticed.

It didn't take a superhero's hearing to hear the voices from the locker room—the most distinctive being a German accent that could only be one guy.

"Maybe he's dating Cam."

Then, there was a quiet ripple of laughter.

Kevin stopped dead in his tracks, his eyebrows rising. He looked behind him, but Fisher had headed to the other ice to join Coach Walker.

He looked back towards the locker room entrance, his hands curling tighter into his gloves.

"You know, he gets a little one-on-one mentoring from his hometown boy..." Hans snickered.

There was no way Hans could be talking about anyone else.

He'd expected this moment years ago. Years of walking into locker rooms expecting to be the next one shoved into a locker, or to hear insults in the showers. Figuring someone would look at him one day and just magically *see* the gay under his skin, start spreading these nasty rumors.

For all those years, he'd planned his confrontation: telling the guy he was being a fucking asshole, that it didn't matter who he fucked, that that was none of his business anyway since he was too butt-ugly to be worried about him in the showers with him…

But all that was gone now that he was listening to his roommate talk about him behind his back.

Kevin squared his jaw and walked down the hall, rounding the corner into the locker room.

"Oh, hey," Hans greeted as casually as could be, that usual smile on his face.

Careful as could be to act normal, Kevin returned the smile and clapped his arm on the way by to the locker. "I'm team red."

Hans was team yellow. It'd be a shame if a practice fight broke out.

No, don't think that way. Kevin couldn't afford to fuck things up, even if only with a reserve team member. He had to be the bigger man until he figured out what the fuck to do.

Nobody believed those rumors, did they?

A quick glance around at the guys changing practice jerseys as they split into teams told him nothing. Nobody was really paying either him or Hans any mind… or they were embarrassed at getting caught gossiping. At least the chuckles he'd heard seemed too few for the number of guys in here.

Kevin raised a hand in a quick wave and headed out of the locker room.

Can't fuck up a third time.

That was the refrain in Kevin's head. Today had already given him two big fuck-ups, right in front of Coach Walker's face. Once, he'd turned the wrong way during a drill, almost taking out a line of his fellow players. The second time, he'd almost tripped during crossover drills and Coach Walker had told him off.

Really stupid, rookie shit. The kind of shit that got you laughed at or sent home, and Kevin wasn't sure which was worse.

He had to focus. Hans didn't matter, really. If he was a homophobic dick, whatever… Kevin could confront him on it and move out. His career mattered a hell of a lot more.

Still, it felt like he'd been sucker-punched, and when Coach Walker pulled him aside, it was all Kevin could do not to let his hands shake.

Not everyone made it through prospects camp.

"Kevin? A word."

He wasn't the first guy Coach Walker had talked to over the last couple days. Some of them left the office looking pleased as punch, and others…

Well, his stomach twisted with nervous anticipation as he followed the coach into his office.

Coach Walker gestured for him to shut the door.

"So," the coach said, stretching out his shoulders as he

leaned on the desk. "Look, I'll keep it short. Your performance is fine so far. You're a fast learner."

Oh, thank God.

That raised an even more uncomfortable possibility, though. Fucking hell, Kevin didn't want to make an *issue* of this.

"Right. Thanks, Coach."

"This is about something else, you probably know what."

Kevin hesitated, then slowly nodded. "Maybe."

"None of us want to know right now if what's being said about you is true. I normally wouldn't even address it," Coach Walker told him bluntly, and he was looking Kevin dead in the eye.

Kevin resisted the urge to look away, blush, shift from foot to foot like he was *guilty* of something. He wasn't, fuck it, and he wasn't gonna let that prick get to him. "Right."

"But Hans has an awful attitude. He's been saying that shit all day where he thinks I'm not gonna hear about it. I think it's because he's jealous you took his spot on the team."

There was rushing in Kevin's ears, but he did his best to ignore it and shifted his weight from one skate to the other. He'd feel a lot more comfortable if they were on ice right now. He could just pirouette away from this conversation on ice. Kevin had a moment of trying not to laugh before he came to his senses.

"Like I said, it's bullshit drama that I don't want to feed. We're not about that around here," Coach Walker told him, his voice crisp. "I'm only telling you because you're living together, and it seems like a precarious situation. Look out for yourself, ask Fisher if you need help finding another place to live, do what you have to do. But don't make this into drama, kid."

Kevin nodded sharply, tugging his gloves off to press against his thigh. "Yes, coach. Thanks, coach."

Coach Walker didn't look unkind as he watched Kevin for a moment, then nodded. "If you want this job, don't let him have it back."

"Yes, sir."

Kevin's voice was louder now, his eyes steely.

Hans wanted to bide his time all summer, then fight dirty now that push came to shove?

Fine. He could play that game.

When Coach Walker nodded for him to go, Kevin almost stomped back out to the ice, his body burning with adrenaline. He was ready to drill until he couldn't drill anymore.

Matty joined him seconds after he stepped onto the ice, stopping by him in a quick spray of ice, then skating alongside him to the end. He was sometimes busy with major league drills, but other times, they had all the prospects together. That meant Kevin got to see him a lot more than he'd expected.

It was also a bit distracting, but Kevin was learning to cope.

"What happened?" Matty asked. "You still in?"

Kevin nodded slightly and muttered, "It's no big deal. Hans is spreading a gay rumor about me." He emphasized the last word slightly. He didn't want Matty feeling like he was in danger, even though...

Well, he was. Anyone close to him was now.

"The bastard," Matty whispered, his gaze cutting around the arena in search of him.

"Hey, whoa," Kevin murmured, tugging his gloves back on and grabbing his stick from the bench while Matty flanked him like a bodyguard about to beat some assholes down.

"Nobody was playing along. I think that's why they're not really talking to him."

"I heard something about that," Matty admitted under his breath. "Just didn't know it was him."

"You could look a little less like you're about to cut a bitch," Kevin snorted.

Matty hesitated, then chuckled as he shifted his stick in his hands and pushed his helmet back on. "Sorry. Yeah."

"It's no big deal," Kevin told him. He didn't want Matty going out and getting trouble started. The best way to make a rumor big was to act like it was legitimate, after all. "It'll blow over as long as I focus on playing well."

Matty looked dubious but hitched his shoulder in a quick shrug. There were too many guys around to really talk about it, but maybe tonight they could catch each other to talk more about it.

They didn't have time to chat more right now; the guys were already being split up for another group drill.

Kevin's muscles burned, but he'd never felt a stronger fire in the pit of his stomach and desire to succeed. He had more than his own neck on the line now. He wanted so badly to prove that Coach Walker's confidence in him was well-placed.

He wanted to deserve to be by Matty's side.

CHAPTER
Twenty~One
MATTY

SHIT. THEY ALL KNOW.

Matty drew a deep breath as he skated around the ice idly to warm up, stretching his legs and arms out before the practice game.

Kevin had been trying to play it cool, but he was more tense than he probably realized, and Matty didn't want to tell him he had good reason to be.

That conversation on Sunday night at the bar? That hadn't come from nowhere. Over the weekend, Hans had been gossiping in everyone's ear about Kevin—maybe about Kevin and Matty, even.

Why? That wasn't fully clear yet, but Matty had his suspicions. If Kevin was right about it, Hans just wanted a spot on the team. He was feeling threatened, which was understandable. But now Kevin was living with the guy.

That worried him.

He cast a quick, sharp look across the ice as they assembled into practice teams. Hans wasn't looking right at him, and he hadn't all day. Now he knew why.

"We're playing a quick, clean game. No stunts. Show me your basic skills," Coach Walker was calling out as the guys skated closer to him, assembling for the pre-game talk. "We'll be trying out a few combinations of lines, so stay on your toes. If we need to pause, we'll do it, but we'll try to play straight through and do a breakdown later. If we break, don't wander off. The sooner we finish, the better. Once we're done, stick around and we'll assign you to massages, physio, whatever you need done, or send you home."

There was a murmur of agreement.

"I didn't hear you," Coach Walker told them.

"Yeah!" Matty called out, brandishing his stick in both hands above his head to a ripple of laughter.

"Thanks, Matty. Glad you're on top of your game. Okay, pay attention. First lines, everyone…"

Matty wasn't surprised to find himself on the first line, along with Fisher. Just like old days. Only difference was a couple of the new guys were joining them. Coach Walker and the others—their manager, the trainers, and so on—were definitely running field tests.

The first couple minutes of play were more about figuring out each other's styles, and everyone played a careful, defensive game rather than making bold moves without knowing who would back them up. That style didn't suit Matty at all. He chafed without knowing who had his back when he went deep.

It was a relief to be yanked a couple minutes later so he could watch the other guys intently and get more a feeling for the ones he didn't already know. He tried to ignore the chatting from other guys who weren't taking this opportunity as seriously as him.

He only had a couple minutes' rest at a time, though,

since Coach Walker kept sending him back out in different lines—several times with major league players who might actually be on his line, and other times with minor league players.

Including, most recently, Kevin. Kevin was a joy to play with—sharp and attentive, ballsy, but not as bold as Matty. He was too easily squeezed out, but he could work on that. He was lightning-fast and seemed to read Matty's mind more than once, though. Those were major advantages.

When Coach Walker called Kevin off the ice to swap him, Matty caught the flash of frustration on Kevin's face and hid his smile. Yeah, it sucked, but the newbies had to earn their minutes one play at a time. Kevin hadn't been the top of the draft. Not the bottom, but not the kind of guy who got into the first line first thing.

Just like Matty, he'd have to work his way up, but Matty was certain Kevin had a chance.

As long as that asshole didn't try to bring media attention down on him.

"Hey, don't touch me."

"You touched me."

Chris and CJ were mock-shoving each other, chest-bumping and pushing each other up against the boards, pretending to fight.

Then a couple other guys joined in. They were all taking playshots at each other, but the punches and shoves and elbows were relatively light and a couple of them were laughing. Matty stayed out until Hans skated towards the fight, then approached. Matty got his arm around CJ to try to yank him back out of the fray, but Hans broke between them and took a playshot at his shoulder with a grin.

Matty counted him as a friend before. This wouldn't be

out of the ordinary for a couple guys horsing around, but now he wondered.

"Fuck off," he told Hans and shoved him right back.

Hans grabbed Matty's jersey to haul him close, then punched his side a couple times, his hits still light enough to be playful.

Then Matty was almost off-balance, shoved up against the board as Hans rubbed the palm of his glove—a sweaty and gross insult, at best—down his face.

Matty gritted his teeth and took a swing at Hans, not holding back this time, but Hans laughed and sidestepped him nimbly, giving him one more hip check back into the boards. "Missed me." Then Hans shoved him, grabbing his arm and leg to try to pull him off-balance—an even bigger dick move.

That's it.

Matty grabbed Hans's helmet strap to keep him in place, then sucker-punched him so fast Hans almost didn't see it coming.

Arms were around him, hands pulling both of them apart, but Matty still saw red. If he hadn't been yanked back, he would have been breaking Hans's face right about now, and from the way Hans worked his mouthguard around as he stared back at him, Hans felt just the same.

But nobody stepped in to back Hans up, and Hans knew it. He was glancing around, his expression deepening into a scowl. He'd lost, and he knew it.

"Hey, hey." That was Fisher, squeezing between them and shoving him roughly towards the bench. "Go sit down for a couple. Take a breather."

"I'm fine." Matty sucked his mouth guard back into place and cracked his neck. "Ready to play."

He didn't want to look over at Kevin. From the bench, Kevin's eyes were boring into him, and Matty had the distinct feeling Kevin was pissed at him for taking matters into his own hands.

Whatever. Hans had always had it coming.

Matty managed to avoid Kevin until after their massages and physio appointments, but they were both wrapped up with that at the same time.

"Kevin, Matty, you guys wanna do autographs together?" Fisher asked. "Watch out for him, Matty," he added with a smirk. "There's a bunch of women that'd like to eat him alive…"

Kevin's cheeks flushed, which made them both laugh along with a couple of other guys.

"Sure," Matty laughed. "Come on."

Just before they approached the arena door, though, Kevin pulled him aside, his smile vanishing. "Dude. Hans is out there right now. You gotta tell me. What the fuck was Hans's problem?"

"He was itching for a fight, that's all." Matty shrugged. "It happens."

"Even teammates?"

"Dude, fights go from *haha, you loser* to *fuck you and your mom* in ten seconds sometimes. It happens," Matty repeated firmly, but Kevin's eyes were still crinkled with worry.

"He knows."

Matty shook his head slightly. He couldn't deny it, though—Hans had been watching Matty head off to the gym with him every day, and now he was certain Hans had come to watch them train together.

Eugh. It left him feeling almost slimy, having that gross asshole watching them for signs of more than friendship.

"Fine, but he can't do shit," Matty murmured, catching Kevin's eyes. "He's just jealous of what you and I have."

Kevin's eyes flickered between Matty's, his brow furrowing with the question. Matty could already read it: *you and I each, or... you-and-I, like both of us?* Then, the answer, as Kevin's face cleared up. *Ohhh. Both.* And then, a blush.

Fuck, he was adorable. However good he was at a stony expression on the ice, he was so easy to read the rest of the time. Matty tried not to laugh.

"Right," Kevin said, clapping his hands together and rubbing. He turned for the arena door. "Let's do this."

Matty followed Kevin out of the arena, grinning at the burst of cheers as they emerged. He had been expecting a couple dozen people at most, but there had to be fifty or sixty here, and it was the end of a training day. Holy shit, these fans had patience.

"Hey, guys," Matty greeted. "Weather been all right?"

"Gorgeous out here," someone answered as Matty approached, holding out a pen for him to sign his autograph. "How's training?"

"I love it," Matty answered honestly. He knew his face was lighting up with enthusiasm. "Been here a few times. Kevin here's new, though."

"Kevin?" someone called out.

"Yeah, that's me," Kevin answered, looking startled.

Oh, man, Kev. People knowing your name is the least of it. Matty laughed. "Yeah, he's doing great too. Loving it. Coach

Walker's great as always. And it's good to see old buddies again." He signed his name almost unconsciously now, pleased to notice a few people looking for Kevin's autograph, too.

Kevin hardly seemed to know what to do, but he got faster after a couple signatures and chatted briefly with a couple fans who asked him what it was like so far.

Soon, they'd all be getting training in how to handle the media, what to say and what not to do, that kind of stuff. For now, this was Kevin's first exposure to a taste of fame.

Some guys played for a love of the sport, others for a love of money, and for those who fit neither camp, this was the moment that cemented their determination to succeed. Fame was a powerful draw.

Still, Kevin stayed humble. Every time someone asked him to sign an autograph, he looked surprised, then pleased.

They hardly noticed Hans head back inside. Once they'd been out there for fifteen minutes or so, another couple guys came out. There were louder cheers for Fisher, and Matty laughed.

"Hey, man," Fisher greeted, coming up between them and putting one arm around each of them, then posing for a couple photos as they all grinned. Then he clapped their shoulders. "You guys heading home?"

"Yeah, I'm wiped," Matty admitted. "Kev?"

"Yeah, me too." Kevin slapped Fisher's back lightly. "I think your fans are waiting." There were people calling Fisher's name to try to get his attention, after all.

Matty smirked. "Go strut your stuff," he teased his buddy, who shoved him. "You gonna be home later?"

"Yep," Fisher promised. "Maybe supper. Kevin, you wanna come over too?" Matty's chest swelled with gratitude that he hadn't had to be the one to make that offer in public.

Kevin looked startled for a moment, and Matty tensed slightly. *Come on, man. Don't go home to Hans.* Then Kevin obviously realized why Fisher had offered and nodded quickly. "Yeah, that'd be great. I'll catch a ride home with you?"

"Of course," Matty answered and pulled back from Fisher. "See you in a couple."

"See you, man."

They raised their hands to wave again, and then they were stepping back inside, changing and waiting for the cab ride home. Leaving in a taxi was a little safer than trying to get home on the bus after a higher-profile day like this, and Matty hadn't driven. He probably would tomorrow.

"You don't mind me coming over?" Kevin asked as they leaned in the side hall, waiting for the text message from the taxi.

Matty shook his head. "Course not." He tried not to flush with heat. Fuck, his roommates wouldn't be much longer before they got home, and then Jasmine had to be walked… Besides, he hadn't been acting out there when he said he was exhausted.

But Kevin was leaning just a couple feet away from him, his bangs in his eyes, those wide eyes so sweet and hopeful as they locked on Matty's.

Matty jolted with relief when the phone vibrated in his hand, giving them both a distraction. "Oh, taxi's here."

They kept a little personal space when they headed through the crowd and found their way to the taxi, then climbed in with another wave each before they pulled off.

Matty leaned forward and gave his address, then closed his eyes to rest them for the quick drive home.

It turned out Kevin was feeling pretty low-key himself.

He ambled up the sidewalk after Matty once the taxi dropped them off outside Matty's house, hands tucked in his hoodie pockets. If only that didn't look so cute, too.

Ugh. Matty really needed to stop thinking of him that way.

In the end, Matty barely remembered the evening—letting Jasmine run around the yard for a while as they all ordered in pizza, watching some shitty movie with their group all half-asleep and aching from head to toe.

"Wanna crash here for the night?" Matty finally offered around a yawn as he stretched, realizing he couldn't keep his eyes open if he tried.

Kevin grimaced. "If you wouldn't mind. I don't wanna face him again yet."

"Don't," Matty agreed. "Come on."

He'd expected more tension when he led Kevin upstairs to his bedroom, but instead, they both quietly stripped off to their boxers and crashed into the bed. Kevin did scoot over to the unused side of the bed, arranging pillows under his head before he breathed out a long sigh.

Matty pushed his face into the pillow and moaned his relief as he started to drift off almost instantly.

"Thanks, man." The voice was just loud enough to get his attention.

Matty's chest warmed as he turned his cheek and squinted at Kevin through the darkness. Then, he reached out, groping carefully under the sheets until he made contact with a firm shoulder. "Course." He squeezed it.

Kevin offered him a smile, his eyes fluttering closed as he breathed out slowly.

Matty didn't even remember letting go of Kevin.

CHAPTER
Twenty~Two

KEVIN

KEVIN KEPT HIS GROANS AS MUFFLED AS HE COULD, stretching slowly in bed as he tried to ease the stiffness out of his body. Thank God for the massage yesterday, or it would have felt like he'd been hit by a train.

Instead, it just felt like he'd been hit by a speed skater, which was about right.

He idly ground his morning wood into the mattress underneath, half-wondering if he wanted to be lazy and jerk off here, or wait for the shower…

Then, he caught his breath, his eyes flying open.

Shit, he was at Matty's place, and Matty was sleeping soundly next to him.

That ruled *that* idea out… as hot as it was.

Kevin quietly rolled out of bed and stepped into his old clothes, making his way to the bathroom. Once he found a stack of towels and washcloths, he undressed and took a quick shower.

And, while he was at it, enjoyed the company of his hand. With Kevin's head rolled back and his mouth open to gasp for breath, he just about swallowed a load of shower water when he came to the mental image of fucking Matty into the mattress.

Once the high faded and the shower was clean again, he stepped out to towel off and dress in yesterday's clothes. It wasn't like that was a big deal—he'd only worn them to and from the arena anyway.

Shit. He had to confront Hans after practice today, so he could get into his own damn house again.

Fisher was downstairs moments after him, humming cheerily. "Hey! Good morning. Cereal's in there, milk's in the fridge, or do you want a protein shake? I'm making one."

"A shake would be awesome. Thanks," Kevin nodded.

"No problem." Fisher dumped a bag of frozen spinach and berries into the blender, then some milk. He eyed Kevin over the blender. "How's camp going for you?"

Kevin blew out a quiet sigh and shrugged. "Um... good? I want to do better, but I'm not sure what to do."

"Asking is half the battle," Fisher half-smiled. "So I was talking to Coach Walker about you, actually."

Kevin's heart lurched as he pulled out a stool to wait for breakfast. "Right?"

"Yeah. You're a damn hard worker. That beats being some natural genius nine times out of ten. The ones who ride on their talent alone without lifting a damn finger to keep in shape all summer..." Fisher rolled his eyes and slammed the "on" button on the blender, then called out over it, "will wind up going home and eating schnitzel all day."

That made Kevin laugh, at least. He let go of a breath he didn't know he'd been holding. "Thanks," he added. "So... I'm good?"

"As you were? Of course." Fisher smiled at him, then waggled his eyebrows. "Pancakes?"

Kevin laughed with surprise as Fisher beamed and flipped the pan towards himself, brandishing it over the stove. "Fuck, yeah."

Thank God these guys had his back. He just had to be sure not to let them down.

HANS DIDN'T EVEN LOOK AT MATTY ALL DAY. ALL DAY, DOZENS of guys playing and drilling and horsing around together, and Hans managed to avoid being within ten feet of Matty at any given time.

It was actually kind of impressive, as much as it amused Matty.

The only thing that sobered him up was that Kevin didn't seem to be looking at him much, either. Kevin still chatted with him in the morning as they all split the car ride to the arena, and he wasn't actively *avoiding* him, but he also seemed to have his mind on other things.

Matty tried not to stress about it. After all, the guy was still brand new. Kevin was supposed to be focusing on the prospect camp, getting to know the coaches and making sure his spot on the roster was safe.

But would it kill him to give him one of those slow, sweet smiles now and then?

Matty was on edge with nerves himself, but he threw himself into practice all day, doing everything the coaches asked of him and more. The main coach of his new major league team, Coach Keller, was gonna be a lot fuckin' tougher to impress, Matty figured out quickly.

The drills were even more intense for the half of the guys fighting for a chance on the major league team. From break-outs to transitioning and offensive zone work, moving back into defensive zones, the individual elements of the game seemed to be a lot more important to the staff at this level. There were no more practice games for Matty and the other guys today.

And as opposed to Kevin's level, where the staff seemed to be focusing on teaching skills, there were a lot more business decisions going on every moment on the other side of the glass when Matty and the guys were on the ice.

Matty could see tentative rosters being drawn up as their day progressed. All he could hope was that he was on them by the end of this week. He was working and putting every-thing he had into it, so if that wasn't good enough, he'd just have to work some more.

"Hey," Matty greeted when Kevin joined him in the locker room to unlace his skates, his head down. He nudged Kevin's elbow with his own to get his attention. "How was today?"

Kevin blew out a sigh, those wonderful pink lips pursing as he gave an expressive eye roll. "Can't tell. I'm just doing what they tell me to."

Mmm. That wasn't what Fisher said.

Fisher seemed excited to have Kevin on the team—he'd told Matty twice that day that Kevin was impressing everyone with his learning speed and willingness to work his ass off to be as good as everyone else, or better. But he wouldn't spoil that surprise for Kevin.

Then there was one other conversation he'd had with Fisher that morning that he had to bring up with Kevin.

"You're fine," Matty said instead, watching Hans head out of the locker room on his way home. His gaze turned back to Kevin. "Hey, man, we should talk about that."

Kevin jerked his head in a quick nod, stepping out of his skates and rolling his shoulders. "I need to go home sooner or later."

"Fisher and I wanna give you a ride home."

Kevin thought about it for a moment, pulling off his shoulder pads. "Won't the people waiting outside think it's weird?"

Matty snorted. "Nah. Hans hasn't been bringing shit up with them. I searched on Twitter." No gossip going around like there no doubt would be if Hans had spilled anything.

"Right," Kevin murmured under his breath, watching a couple other guys play-fighting on the other side of the locker room. "Yeah. If you think it's not weird."

"Not at all," Matty told him. More importantly, he didn't want Hans putting Kevin out of commission somehow. He grabbed his towel and headed to the shower, not thinking twice about being naked even around Kevin right now. His body was too sore to think about fucking that cute little ass.

Once they had their shit packed up and they were relatively clean, Matty felt a little more human, but he really needed food. He waited until Fisher was done, then headed out with both Fisher and Kevin for another round of autographs before they fled for Matty's car.

"Does that ever get weird?" Kevin asked. "Does it happen through the season?"

"There's more of it now than during the season, but yeah, it's kinda weird sometimes. It's not like being an actor, but you have this core group of fans who will follow you in the grocery store," Fisher snorted.

Kevin burst out laughing. "Really?"

"Oh, yeah. You're a public figure now, man," Fisher told Kevin with a grin, glancing sideways at Matty.

"It's true," Matty agreed. "I've run into people in restaurants and malls before who just wanted to talk to me. Sometimes kids. That's nice," he admitted. "You see them getting all hero-worship on you, which is cute. I signed up to talk to the kids' camp…"

"Oh man," Fisher groaned, buckling up as Matty pulled out of the parking space. "You got suckered into that?"

Matty snorted. In reality, he'd approached Coach Walker about it earlier that week and the coach had instantly agreed to pass his name on to the staff. By the end of the day, they'd told him they'd love to have him. "Yeah, press-ganged in," he joked. "It's so hard."

"What's involved?" Kevin asked from the backseat.

"Not a lot, unless you're one of the actual coaching staff. You just go talk to them about the career and what it's like, give a kind of motivational talk. They like to have a couple actual players from the major and minor teams do it, so the kids can see… you know, the potential."

Fisher smirked. "And some players from the women's team for the girls."

I really gotta tell at least him someday. Matty forced a quick laugh and nodded. "It's a good opportunity. Makes you look PR-savvy, too, if your agent wants that."

"My agent does want me getting out more," Kevin admitted.

Fisher looked back at Kevin. "Yeah, you should totally do it, man. I did it before. It's not *that* bad, like he said."

"And also tell me where you live," Matty laughed. "So I can go there."

"Oh yeah." Kevin gave him his address, so Matty leaned forward to punch it into his phone. Only a couple blocks away from him, at least. Then, as Fisher and Kevin talked about the kids' camp, Matty leaned back to focus on driving and plan how he'd break Hans's face if he was a dick.

As it turned out, Hans barely looked at the three of them when they got home. He mumbled a greeting as he grabbed a pop bottle and pizza box from the dining room table to bring to his room.

Fisher shot Matty a look as Hans's door shut, and Matty shrugged and looked at Kevin.

Kevin just grinned and half-shrugged. "Guess we're cool. Thanks, guys."

"Okay. We'll get home, then," Matty concluded. "Text me tonight and tell me how he is."

"Yeah, man." Kevin smiled, his gaze flicking to Matty's lips and back up to his eyes for a moment.

For a crazy moment, he wished he could have a goodbye kiss, but they couldn't very well smack lips in front of their buddy. They just leaned in for a quick half-hug before Kevin hugged Fisher the same way.

Then he and Fisher were off, heading back home and not saying much to each other.

When he got the text, it was simple.

All's fine :) Too busy to worry anyway lol. Thanks for the ride and company.

Matty breathed out a sigh of relief. He was soaking in the

tub, letting a salt bath ease his muscles and keep him tension-free for tomorrow's practice. Walking Jasmine had used up the last few ounces of his energy for the day. He was fine just kicking back in the tub until someone yelled at him to get out of the bathroom.

He wiped off his hands and rested his phone on the edge of the tub as he poked at the screen to text back.

Great. Glad we could help.

A moment later, Kevin added something.

Staying with you was cool. Do that again sometime?

Matty grinned. Kevin had wished they'd been in more of a mood to fool around, too, hadn't he? They only had the rest of this week, the weekend, and the kids' camp week before they were separated again, each heading back to his own hometown.

Oh ya man. Sleepover ;)

ROFL. I signed up for the kids camp btw. My agent wants to kiss me.

Matty shifted, wondering if Kevin was trying to make him jealous or hinting at something here. He finally settled on a neutral response.

:(Hope your agent's cute.

Not as cute as you bro, Kevin told him.

Matty burst out laughing and sent a wink and a quick, *Thanks bro.*

Then his phone rang, and Matty's heart lurched. He half-expected it to be Kevin following up on that flirtation by phone. Fuck, yes, he would have phone sex…

Oh, no. It wasn't Kevin.

He sighed but slid his finger across the screen to answer it, bringing it to his ear and stretching out in the tub again. "Hello?"

"Hey. Is this Matty?"

"It is. Who's this?"

"I'm Henry. Great to talk to you. I wanted a word about the new Fredericton minor league team."

Well, at least he wasn't bullshitting around. Matty leaned forward and pulled the plug on the tub, then bumped his head back against the bathroom wall. "Right… You're the guy who talked to Cam, aren't you?"

"Cameron… Riley?"

"Yeah," Matty confirmed almost aggressively. "You know, the one with the heart problem."

"Right." Henry cleared his throat, sounding slightly sheepish. He had to know Matty was pissed about that. Henry and his buddy, the new team owner, had hounded Cam almost into heart failure from trying so hard to recruit him as their top star. "I wanted to talk to you about where you're going next season."

"This season hasn't even begun yet," Matty snorted. "And you'd have to talk to my agent anyway."

"Well, I wanted a more personal touch. I know you know… some guys from Fredericton—"

"Like Cam."

"—who I'm sure would be delighted to have you around. We've got a great team already moving into town. A few more stars would be fantastic."

Matty rubbed his face. "Right. You still have to get my agent to get back to you, talk to him about the offer."

"Can I count on your support building this new team, making something great in your buddies' hometown?"

Matty crinkled his nose. Now he sounded like a phone bank worker. "Yeah, you do what you gotta do. Call my agent and we'll chat. Have a good one."

He hung up before Henry could interject again, then rolled his eyes as he pulled himself up from the last couple inches of bathwater. He hated being pressured into making a decision, and one like this? Only an idiot would take a PTO contract or something on the spot, and take an enormous pay cut from what he'd just achieved… unless he didn't think he could last the year without being cut from the roster.

And Matty had to hope he could make it.

He ignored his phone and toweled himself off, then wrapped the towel around his waist to head back to his bedroom.

CHAPTER
Twenty~Four
KEVIN

"Good, Kevin! Come off now."

Kevin's legs wanted to give way as he skated around the last obstacle, then over to step off the ice. He wobbled in a way he hadn't done since he stepped off the ice at age three in his first pair of skates.

"Oh, Jesus," he laughed under his breath, jerking his chin in a nod to Coach Walker. "Am I good to change?"

"No. You can do better than that. I want you going once more. Watch how Matty does it."

Kevin could barely remember when the day had begun. Aside from a short lunch break, they'd been put through their paces. He was working harder on the ice than he'd ever worked in his life, and every step of the way, there had been a coach or player development manager or captain or something critiquing him.

Matty was gliding effortlessly across the ice, spinning around each pylon and moving the puck back and forth somehow behind the pylon and around it *without* tripping over either the stick or the puck.

For a second, Kevin kind of hated him, but only because he was jealous. He'd always been told his stick handling abilities were second to none—literally, not as a euphemism, though he wished he'd heard that more too. Now he was watching Matty effortlessly flick the puck between the front and back of his blade, all without tripping over any of the obstacles.

Matty even spun at the end in a quick, sharp stop exactly on the mark, the puck on the tip of his stick and ready to slap into the goal.

Fisher banged the end of his stick against the flooring and a couple other guys joined in, thumping their approval and whooping.

Even Coach Walker smiled. "Perfect," he approved.

Shit.

Matty wasn't just good, he was *great*. Kevin was more nervous than ever. Somehow, Matty was hanging around him? Had he gotten too distracted by Matty and hanging out with him at his cabin and the museum and shit when he should have been training more?

But no guy could stay in the gym 24/7. He had to have a life, too, right?

"Again," Coach Walker instructed Kevin as Matty slid past him, jumping up and off the ice and punching his arm on the way by.

Kevin offered a weak smile and stepped back down again, taking a deep breath as he skated back into position.

This was it. They were gonna find out that he wasn't as good as someone had thought he was. And Hans was right there, willing and waiting to take the job. Hell, all it took was one slip—one little distraction—and he'd be back home looking for a new career.

No. Focus on this. One skate in front of the other.

Kevin drew a breath, then flicked the puck to the inside of his stick and started moving before he could second-guess himself. He moved on pure instinct, trying to go fast enough that his brain couldn't kick in. Muscle memory from doing this exercise three times already, and the instinct of what to do with the puck when he had it. They'd trained on every element of this at some point this week... this just required him to put together the pieces.

Around, his stick looping back and forth, eye on the puck, and then it clicked into place.

It was the state of flow that every athlete wanted, and it sank in as quickly as a sun ray burst from behind a thick, heavy cloud. His brain was light and floating, watching what he did but not really offering input. It was all his body, and the trust he put in himself from skate to stick.

Pass, receive. Pass, receive.

And then he was done, the last pylon already past him. Shit, he had to stop—turn around...

Kevin stopped messily, almost losing his balance as he screeched to a sudden halt. His cheeks flushed as he stopped, his chest heaving for breath.

Matty whooped. "Way better! Sorry, Coach."

Coach Walker shook his head but smiled as he gestured to Kevin. "Come off. Yeah, that was better. Good going, kid."

Kevin did his best to study the other guys who went, but he was still dizzy with excitement from the moment where drills had connected with other drills. By the time they were sent off for physio, skates off and back in sneakers, most of the guys were worn down but enthusiastic.

All around, Kevin could see guys learning and putting together the pieces just like him. *That* was the point of the camp, not just assessing their skill levels right now—seeing how fast and well they could learn.

"Hey," Matty greeted as they collapsed in the bleachers to wait for the physio talk and training session on post-game cool-downs. He was sprawling a couple seats away, all his limbs splayed out every which way.

Kevin glanced around as he answered, "Hey." Nobody else was nearby right now, which made Kevin's heart sink with relief. "How's it going?"

"Better now you're smiling at me." Matty winked at him, and Kevin felt his heart pick up with a little flutter.

No... God, I have to focus. Kevin still turned red and mumbled something like, "Cool."

Matty laughed. "You all right?"

Kevin shrugged and nodded all at once. "I just... it's distracting being 'round you." He kept his voice down in case anyone else came walking their way.

Matty moved over to the seat next to him, folding himself in more neatly. "Yeah. I know. Me, too."

"And we still haven't talked about... all this." Kevin couldn't believe he was bringing this up *now*. He had to be exhausted for his filters to be coming down.

"Yeah." Matty folded his hands in his lap, licking his lips. He looked like he was about to talk to a TV reporter or something.

He's nervous? Kevin smiled a bit. "But we should probably hold off until after the heat's off. Maybe we can hang out, like, before our speech to the kids next week?"

"This weekend?" Matty asked.

Kevin nodded. "We'll figure something out after this week's done." *Assuming neither of us get sent home early, of course.*

"All right." Matty hesitated, glancing around carefully and then looking back at Kevin.

Kevin grabbed Matty's chin in one hand and leaned in for one fast, forceful kiss right against Matty's lips. After a hot second or two of lips sliding, catching each other's lips with their teeth, they pulled apart again.

Holy shit.

That chemistry was back. It was nearly impossible to resist grabbing Matty and hauling him close again, but Kevin rocked himself up to his feet and let out a quick breath. "Right. Physio. I think I hear them starting."

When he looked back over his shoulder, Matty was slowly getting to his feet, staring after him with wide, dazed eyes.

Oh, I'd leave you even more stunned than that if I could.

"Get your asses over here," the physiotherapist, Rick, told them as they rounded the corner. "And put your phones away, guys. No distractions."

No distractions: that was exactly why they had to stay out of each other's pants until this fucking camp was done. No matter how much Kevin wanted to grab Matty and haul him out back to lose every ounce of strained self-control in each other's arms.

CHAPTER
Twenty-Five
RYAN

ALL WEEK, RYAN HAD BARELY HEARD A PEEP FROM KEVIN. IT wasn't surprising, since this was the week of his first training camp, but Ryan was anxious to hear how it was going.

He figured he'd get a call on the weekend to catch up, but he didn't expect to get a call from Kevin right before midnight on Friday, almost Saturday morning. Half-expecting to hear a drunk and happy buddy, Ryan smiled and picked up.

"Hey, Kev."

"Hey," Kevin answered, but there wasn't background chatter from a bar, and Kevin's voice was rough.

Instantly, Ryan's lips drew into a frown and he turned off the TV. "What's up, man?"

"Well, camp week just ended."

Oh, God. Don't let him have been sent home.

"And?" Ryan asked, trying to keep his voice casual and not stress Kevin out more.

"And, uh, looks like I'm still on the roster… pending the actual training camp and stuff, of course. And they're probably gonna give me a couple sheltered minutes here or there of actual game time, slowly build it up."

Ryan exclaimed, "Awesome!"

"Yeah. It's a relief." Still, Kevin didn't sound like he was that relieved. Something else was on his mind. Boy trouble?

Ryan raised a brow. When Kevin didn't say anything, he prompted, "But?"

"Um…" Kevin hedged.

"Dude, you don't call in the middle of the night without a reason." It wasn't that late, but Kevin sounded like he'd just been asleep. "Spill," Ryan told him simply.

"I really, really like this guy. Shit, I just don't know what comes next."

Ryan hummed under his breath. "You hinted at that before. What happened?"

"I…" Kevin trailed off, then cleared his throat. "Someone's trying to gossip about us, and it's complicated, what with hockey and things…"

"It involves hockey? You want me to add Cam to this call? He knows the league better than me."

Kevin sounded relieved. "Yes, please. Three-way call? What is this, the 90s?"

"Wait for it," Ryan laughed. "Uh, hold on… do you know how?"

"No. Do you?"

"No. Hold on," Ryan told Kevin. "I'll Google it."

He pulled up his laptop and Googled *how to 3way call*. After a few button presses, he managed to find the right key combination, then added Cam's phone number.

They both listened quietly to the ringing phone, and then Cam answered, his voice husky. "Hey, what's up Ryan?"

"I got Kevin on the phone."

"No shit. Hey, Kev!" Cam answered, already sounding more awake. "How's it going, man?"

"Great," Kevin answered. "They kept me around. Coach Walker seems to think I'm all right. It's not about hockey, actually. Well, it sort of is..."

Cam hummed, his voice even and calm. "This about dating?"

"How'd you know?"

"Lucky guess." Something shifted in the background and then thumped. "Okay, just had to grab some fresh air," Cam added, and the sound of the patio door sliding shut faintly echoed through the line. "Okay, what's going on?"

Kevin blew out a quick sigh. "Long story short? There's this guy I like, but as far as the league goes... I don't wanna be out. But my roo—*someone* here... is trying to spread rumors and shit."

Cam grunted a sigh. "Fuck that bullshit."

"I know," Ryan muttered, but he otherwise stayed quiet. Cam had the hockey side covered, which was good since Ryan never knew what to say. He was a lot better at listening than giving advice.

"Yeah," Kevin murmured. "So I'm pretty sure everyone knows about me now, and I haven't even formally practiced with the team yet..."

Cam interrupted before Kevin could get panicky. "It's fine. Dude, I was only half-in the closet the whole time. Everyone knew. The guys are great. If you date a fan or whatever, like I did... as long as he isn't an asshole like *him*... they'll look after you."

"He's... not a fan."

Cam sucked in a quick breath and even Ryan muffled his gasp.

Oh, boy. Kevin was dating a hockey player.

"Going right in the deep end, huh? A player?" Cam chuckled quietly. "Tell me it ain't a coach."

Kevin sounded sheepish. "Yeah. A player."

"Who better to understand the life, though?" Cam followed up instantly and Ryan grunted in agreement.

"Or we could both get distracted by each other and fuck up each other's careers."

Cam snorted with laughter and Ryan crinkled his eyes, waiting for the punchline. "Dude," Cam told Kevin. "Are you with him 24/7? You still hitting the gym? Making all your practices?"

"Uh, yeah."

"Calm the shit down then, bro."

Ryan snorted with laughter, too. "Yeah, he's kind of right. What exactly's the problem? He on your team? Can't focus on the puck when he's there?"

"No, no, not at all. M—He's, uh, he's... on the major league team."

Cam whistled teasingly, and Ryan could picture Kevin's cheeks turning beet red. "Friends in high places, then," he teased. "Seriously, dude. It's chill. Guys secretly date all the time. We just don't talk about it."

"Seriously?"

"Yeah," Cam laughed. "I've known a lot of guys I think were fucking, or at least making out heavily."

Ryan chuckled, then told Kevin, "See? I figured he'd know what he was talking about."

"All right, all right," Kevin laughed, but his voice was a little lighter now. "You don't think it'll be a big deal?"

"If it gets to the media and the public, if it blows up," Cam told him, "you two will have to be ready for that. If you become a *you two*, that is. Just… play really hard. Keep proving you deserve to be there. Cause if it comes out, you'll have to be twice the player anyone else has to be to get support, and that's shitty, but…"

"Yeah," Kevin murmured. "Yeah, I figured."

Cam was quiet for a few moments, and when he spoke up, his voice was quiet. "You're lucky to play with him—even if not quite *with* him—though. You're practicing at the same rinks, you'll see each other playing at home, in parties… especially during the summer. Make the most of that."

Ryan wondered how hard it had been on Cam to date someone outside the hockey life. From what he knew, Cam's ex was a dirtbag anyway. He hoped Kevin had better taste.

"Right," Kevin said.

"And bring him out here for me to meet, Jesus," Cam laughed. "This summer, have him come home with you or something."

"But that'd look—" Kevin started.

"Totally normal, too. Remember what's normal in the hockey world—bromances are, like, a *thing* all over the league. You can get away with murder, dude. More than outside hockey, really."

"Huh," Kevin hummed. "Yeah… I might. Okay. Thanks, guys. I should probably hit the hay."

"Course," Ryan spoke up. "I wanna meet the guy too."

"Right," Kevin laughed. "Okay. Good night." After their good nights, Kevin hung up, leaving Ryan wondering if Cam was still there.

"You still there?" Cam asked, just as he was about to.

"Yeah," Ryan laughed. "Thanks for picking that one up, man."

Cam chuckled. "No problem, dude. Glad to put my

ridiculously specialized skill set to work sometimes. Shit, though… I think I know who he likes.”

“No way,” Ryan chuckled. “Is he… all right?”

“Uh…” Cam said, hedging for a moment, then sighed. “I think so. I’m kinda worried for them both, if it’s who I think it is. But there’s nothing I can do from out here. But yeah, I’d trust that guy with my own brother.”

“I’ll keep working on him if you do,” Ryan promised. “Make sure they come out for a visit.”

“Good,” Cam laughed. “We’ll see ‘em by the end of the summer, then. Okay, I gotta get to bed before Noah comes to find me.”

“Right,” Ryan chuckled quietly, glancing over towards his own dark, empty bedroom. Fuck, he’d been right: he *was* gonna end up the last single one.

“Take care, all right? Still on for a barbecue this weekend?”

“Still on,” Ryan promised. “See you, man.”

“Good night.”

When Ryan pushed through his jealousy, he was glad for Kevin. Hockey would be a damn lonely life and career if he didn’t find someone. He just wondered how long Kevin’s deal with this new guy could stay in the shadows, especially if his roommate was being an asshole.

At least he didn’t have *that* problem. On the other hand, sometimes he’d kill to live with someone just so he had someone to talk to at night.

“Bedtime,” he said out loud. He had some projects to build this weekend, and the table saw didn’t care how much sleep he’d gotten.

CHAPTER

Twenty~Six

KEVIN

RESTAURANT TONIGHT?

Kevin hoped Matty was still up for it. It had been a couple painful days without talking much—just a couple words in passing as they rushed about, doing everything that was asked of them. Matty had looked worried and distracted the whole while, or perhaps just focused on training. He didn't know him well enough yet to tell the difference.

He set his phone down on the coffee table as he cleared the empty pop cans, beer bottles, and food wrappers off the coffee table. Before he could carry the bag to the kitchen, his phone went off with a reply from Matty.

Kevin nearly lurched across the table, banging his knees on the edge. He cursed but swiped to see the message.

Sure! Meet at the bus stop?

Okay! 6?

Works for me :)

Matty's emoticon made Kevin grin. He sent a smile back, then pocketed his phone. If there was the possibility of Matty coming back, he wanted the place looking nice.

With Hans always in the wrong fucking place at the wrong fucking time, though… He was out right now, but he might be back tonight, and Kevin didn't want to push his luck. Kevin grimaced, eyeing the trash bag. No way they could come over here, then.

Oh, well. Kevin would keep cleaning anyway. If worst came to worst, it would make moving out faster.

***

"Hey, stranger."

Matty's voice echoed as Kevin rounded the corner to the bus stop. It wasn't hard to spot him, leaning against the glass and dressed in a forest green shirt that brightened his eyes and set off his brilliant white smile.

"Hi," Kevin answered as he approached him, mirroring that smile. He was still aching a little from the week, but constant massages and physiotherapy had helped stave off the worst of it. "How's it going?" Suddenly, he felt underdressed in his blue checked shirt and black trousers, but Matty's eyes gave an appreciative flick up and down his body.

"Not bad." Matty reached out to push his arm lightly. "Hey, you did awesome at camp."

Kevin brightened up instantly. "Thanks. You think?"

"Oh, yeah. You'll be on first line in a season or two," Matty smiled.

Kevin rolled his eyes and shoved Matty back. "Don't pull my leg."

"I'm not!" As the bus approached, Matty leaned in, his breath ghosting over Kevin's ear as he murmured, "I'll pull something else, though."

Kevin's eyebrows shot up as he watched Matty step onto the bus, then jolted into action to follow him. That was fuckin' bold.

Ooh, it got him hot under the collar, though.

"Where we going?" Matty asked once they found seats.

"Italian?" Kevin suggested. He knew just the place—it was massive and airy, with lots of romantic touches like lamps. Best of all, a disused railcar inside had been turned into seating. He'd made a reservation, hoping to get a table in there.

Matty grinned. "Mm. Sounds good. Are we gonna have a Lady and the Tramp moment?"

Kevin laughed and bumped his knee against Matty's in a light shove. "Shut up." That kinda sounded hot, though… if it weren't for the public thing.

"Ooh, you want to," Matty teased.

Kevin's cheeks heated up and he cleared his throat. "Anyway, how was the rest of your week?"

Something flickered behind Matty's eyes, but he shrugged it off. "Good, I guess. Just work and sleep."

"You sure?" Kevin frowned. "You looked a bit stressed this week. I mean, if it's just prospects camp…"

"Yeah, that was stressful, too," Matty agreed, hesitating and looking around before he looked back at Kevin. "Uh, had to talk to my agent about my future plans."

Kevin winced. "That sounds fun."

"Yeah. Someone approached and offered… well, a spot on the new Fredericton team."

"No shit," Kevin murmured, his eyebrows shooting up. "Really? Wait, wait, is that… the same one that they were talking about last year? That was talking to Cam?"

"Same guy, even," Matty agreed, rolling his eyes and scoffing. "I told him to fuck off and talk to my agent, but…

you know, that's been bouncing round my head. What happens after this season." He was watching Kevin closely, leaving his knee against Kevin's, and Kevin got it: Matty was wondering about *them*, too.

Yeah. If we start dating, that is a pretty big thing.

Kevin licked his lips. "Right. You mean with transfers and stuff. I mean, we can be traded pretty much anytime… bought and sold."

"Dance, monkey, dance?" Matty chuckled quietly, but he reached out to brush Kevin's knee quickly. "But we'll talk that over later, you know?"

"Yeah," Kevin quickly agreed. He'd known in the back of his mind since starting to think about doing more with Matty that long-distance periods were a certainty, what with away games and all. But this was a pretty permanent long-distance arrangement.

He could just be traded to Florida or Los Angeles or Vancouver or anywhere next year. Or Matty could be sent off just the same. Did that put an expiration date on their relationship?

Kevin licked his lips. He'd done long-distance—with his boyfriend in St. John's, last year, who hadn't lasted long. A couple flights back and forth and that had been it for them. He'd decided back then not to do it again, but this… This was different.

Matty seemed different.

They got to the restaurant and strolled inside, Matty laughing at his choice of place. "Really?" he asked as Kevin gave his last name.

Kevin glanced at him. "Shut up. I love their garlic butter."

"Guess I better have it, too, then," Matty winked. "Or it'll drive me nuts."

"In a good way?"

Matty mocked, *"In a good way? Is there a good way?"*

"I love garlic!" Kevin protested, drawing back from Matty as he followed their waitress to the table. "You don't?"

"I can take it or leave it."

"Wow. This thing is over, man. We can't be friends," Kevin snorted. What kind of madman didn't like garlic butter? Especially from this place? It was legendary.

Matty burst out laughing.

The waitress seated them at an intimate table for two at the end of the boxcar and Kevin beamed at Matty. "Cool, huh? You ever sat in here before?"

"No," Matty admitted, still laughing quietly. "You really like it, huh?"

Kevin shrugged. "Came out here with my parents when I was a kid to see the Hockey Hall of Fame and watch a couple games and stuff… we came here. Fond memories, all right?"

"Awww," Matty teased, but he was smiling as he picked up his menu. "Yeah, my family used to come down here in the summers. Go to the amusement park or the expo, sometimes Niagara Falls."

Kevin chuckled. "We only did once. It's kind of a long drive from New Brunswick, and my parents didn't get a lot of time off work." He fidgeted with the long paper menu, folding and unfolding it. "But I remember that summer really well."

Matty gave him a soft smile, then looked down at the menu.

Kevin stole a second to watch his eyes flicker back and forth across the paper. Matty's hair flopped into his eyes, his unshaven stubble contrasting his neat appearance perfectly. He looked exactly unkempt enough to be sexy, not styleless.

Then he looked down at the menu, forcing himself to choose something instead of ogling his buddy.

Once they'd placed their orders, Matty started chatting again. It was so fucking easy to talk to Matty. Despite Kevin's nerves and worries, just talking to him always made him relax.

Eventually, the topic came back around to the offer.

"So, you think you're New Brunswick-bound next year?" Kevin asked lightly.

"Nah," Matty shook his head. "It'd be a pretty big step down for me. I mean, man, I made it here. I should be able to stick around if I make enough of an impression."

Kevin nodded. He was still a couple years off from that kind of paycheck and glory, but he could almost imagine it.

"And we still have a year to figure that out," Matty added warmly, offering a quick smile.

Kevin nodded slowly. "In the meantime…"

"Yeah," Matty breathily laughed. "We should figure *this* out."

Kevin fidgeted with nerves. "Um. Maybe not in public?"

A flicker of something passed through Matty's face— disappointment? Frustration? But Matty nodded, offering another quick smile. "Probably good thinking. We haven't really been subtle up to this point."

Kevin laughed quietly. "I wanna have more time alone with you. My stupid roommate will probably be around tonight, though." *Fucking Hans. Ugh.*

"No problem. The other guys are all gone tonight at my place," Matty told him, his eyes fixed on Kevin's as he groped for his glass. He bumped into it, almost knocking it over, and blushed as he grabbed it to set it upright, then sipped his water. "Um, if you want to come over, that is."

"Yeah," Kevin agreed instantly. "I'd like that."

By the end of their garlic bread, salad, pasta, and cheesecake, he was just about full and high off life. Matty made him laugh almost constantly. He was always quick-witted, but patient enough to wait for Kevin to think of interesting topics sometimes, too.

Kevin paid before Matty could reach for his wallet, then led him out of the restaurant, waving off Matty's thanks. "No problem."

"There's the bus. If we run we can make it," Matty laughed.

Somewhere mid-block, Kevin wound up grabbing Matty's hand to pull him along after him. He dropped Matty's hand when they got to the back of the bus lineup just in time, his cheeks hot as he quickly glanced at Matty.

Matty was just grinning back at him, his gaze warm and affectionate.

God, Matty seemed to have no fear in public. Kevin took a breath and let it out, then offered a quick smile back before boarding the bus.

They didn't say anything for the bus ride back, but Kevin was intensely aware of every spot where Matty's knee or thigh bumped his own, and the way Matty's shoulder nestled into his own like Matty wasn't trying to keep to his own space.

When they got off at the usual stop, Matty's arm slid around Kevin's shoulder.

Oh, man, he smelled good. Kevin tried not to sniff at the faint coconut smell he picked up—body wash? Shampoo? It was delicious in combination with whatever light, fresh cologne or aftershave he was wearing. There was no faster way to make him hot than smelling really nice, and crushed up against Matty's hot body, Kevin was already almost uncomfortably warm.

Thank God they were so close to Matty's place.

"That *was* a good meal," Matty admitted with a grin as he steered Kevin down the street at a casual amble.

Kevin slipped his own arm around Matty's waist, curling his fingers around Matty's hipbone through his shirt and jeans and trying not to overthink it. "Yeah. I liked it."

"I liked the company the best, though," Matty admitted quietly, winking at him. "You get really enthusiastic about things."

"So do you," Kevin chuckled, bumping into Matty's side.

Matty shoved him in return, so Kevin pushed him again, then laughed when Matty grabbed him around the waist to try to hoist him over his shoulder.

"Hey, no, you can't just…!" Kevin laughed, trying to dance around the signpost and Matty at the same time. He barely escaped by squeezing past Matty, bolting down the sidewalk and up the path to Matty's front door. Of course, he had to wait to be let in then.

Matty strode after him at his own pace, and when Kevin turned to catch his eyes, he suddenly couldn't breathe.

Matty was stalking up to the door, keys in his hand, perfectly aware that Kevin had to wait for him. He looked like a predator stalking his next catch. Kevin's whole body flushed with heat, and he slid a hand into his pocket to adjust himself.

Just looking at Matty looking at him like that got him hard. Or maybe that had been the quick grind against Matty's front to escape from the possible headlock.

Fucking hurry up.

Matty brushed past him to lean in and unlock the front

door, then held the screen door open for Kevin to squeeze past him again. "Aprés vous."

The little purred "r" rolling off his tongue sent another shiver down Kevin's spine. He kicked off his shoes, glancing around the dark house and looking for a light switch.

Matty pushed into the foyer behind him, his arm sliding around Kevin's waist as he flicked the switches near Kevin's shoulder, then pushed him up against the wall, grinding against his ass for a moment.

Kevin moaned, rolling his head back against Matty's shoulder as he ran his hand over the back of Matty's. Fuck, he *wanted* him.

"Should we head to my room?"

"We better," Kevin agreed with a breathless laugh. "No chance they're coming home?"

"Nope. They're all gone drinking or seeing family and friends and shit," Matty murmured. "And I might have threatened them to stay out on pain of torture."

"What kind?" Kevin breathily laughed, grinding against that hard cock he could feel pushing into him from behind. The hitched breathing in Matty's throat was very satisfying.

"Pranks. I'm the master. They don't dare fuck with me," Matty murmured. His hand slid slowly down Kevin's stomach towards his groin and Kevin's whole body lit up with fiery desire.

When Matty palmed his cock, Kevin gritted his teeth and hissed, his hips bucking forward into the touch. "Yes…"

"Bedroom?"

"Fuck." Kevin wanted to strip off here, but he supposed he could wait another twenty seconds if he *had* to.

Matty hooked a finger through his belt loop and kept him close as they headed up the stairs to the bedrooms, bypassing a couple closed doors for the open one at the end—Matty's room.

"Jesus," Kevin breathed out when he got to the room, turning to kick the door shut behind Matty and grab him by the cheeks for the rough kiss he'd been craving for goddamn *days* now.

"Mmm," Matty murmured with a deep chuckle. His lips moved slowly and sweetly, exploring and tasting Kevin.

And yeah, Kevin tasted that garlic butter.

He pulled back to laugh shortly, his heart hammering in his chest as Matty walked him backwards toward the bed, guiding him each step of the way.

"What?"

"The fucking bread."

"See?" Matty smirked. "But you taste like it, too. We're even."

Kevin ran his hand up Matty's chest, enjoying the smooth ripple of abs and pecs under his hand. Matty was so fucking solid, like a tree. A sex tree. Shit, he wanted to climb him like one. "Fair enough."

He sprawled backwards onto the bed, rolling his head back against the pillow as Matty followed close against his body, blanketing him instantly with his weight.

Oh, God, that was incredible. Kevin's whole body burned with need as he wrapped his arms around Matty's shoulders, rubbing his hand down his spine to the small of his back and arching into him.

And Matty was there, soothing his anxious need by pressing their lips together in quick, hard kisses.

Kevin had been waiting too fucking long to get Matty into bed to let him keep that up for long. He squeezed

Matty's ass and kneaded, rubbing his thumbs into that wonderful firmness before smacking it lightly.

Matty broke the kiss to laugh hoarsely, his eyes sparkling with surprise. He mouthed at Kevin's jaw, dragging his lips slowly along the stubble until Kevin involuntarily twitched under him. "So sensitive."

"Shut up," Kevin growled.

Matty shook his head. "Not when I can milk this, dude." He nipped Kevin's lower lip, sucking it between his lips slowly and darting his tongue across it.

Kevin was already so raw and on-edge that the slightest teasing—let alone Matty's hand roaming up under his shirt and fidgeting with his nipple—had him gasping for breath. He *was* sensitive, and Matty was like a kid at Christmas every time he found another of his hot buttons.

"Oooh, you like that," Matty purred, his face lighting up again in an impossibly cute grin considering the steaminess of the moment. He pinched Kevin's nipple just hard enough to make Kevin rasp a combination of a gasp and a moan.

"Fucking *hell*, Matty."

Matty snickered, sitting back on his heels at last to unbutton Kevin's shirt and shove it off his arms. He followed suit with his own.

God, his chest was a sight to behold up close—solid as a board, all tight muscle. The primal part of Kevin's brain *loved* it. Drawn to him like a college boy to cheap beer, Kevin couldn't stop his hands from running up his chest, half in awe.

"You'll look like this next year," Matty promised with a grin. "You're almost there yourself, good-looking." And then he tweaked Kevin's nipple again.

Heat flushed through Kevin's cheeks—more than was already burning through his stomach, making his muscles tense as his cock screamed for attention. "Yeah, yeah," he muttered. "We can get back to the kissing part. Or one better."

"I was thinking more than a blowjob tonight—"

Kevin didn't even let Matty finish the sentence. He grabbed Matty's thigh and ran his hand up to the bulge, rubbing with the heel of his palm as Matty's head rolled back and he grunted with pleasure. "Fuck. Yeah. What's taken us so long?"

"Being worried about shit?" Matty laughed under his breath when he could manage it, running a hand down his face and then cupping Kevin's cheek to kiss him.

Kevin loved making him lose his mind, if only for a few moments, too. He murmured against Matty's lips, "Don't think about that right now. Just fuck me."

If he thought about fucking his senior teammate—not even teammate, technically, but a guy *actually* out of his league…

Well, it'd be his turn for him to lose his shit.

"Fuck." Matty's hands were at his zipper, unbuttoning his jeans and sliding them down his hips and thighs at the same time as his underwear. Damn it. He'd chosen his favorite boxer briefs to impress Matty, too.

Kevin's cock sprang free, thick and hard against his stomach as Matty trapped it between their stomachs and ground slowly.

"Yes," Kevin whispered, just about ripping Matty's jeans apart and off. As Matty shifted and squirmed to get his clothes off, Kevin enjoyed that thick cock bobbing in the air above him like a promise.

He couldn't *wait* to take it inside him. All his shower fantasies were coming true.

Then Matty grabbed a condom and lube, and Kevin licked his lips, pressing his feet into the bed. "Hngh."

His chest was tightly-coiled with focused desperation, like they were breaking away down the ice; the goal was in sight and the game rode on this.

Well, not exactly. He'd had colorful fights but never a couple fingers sliding into him during a game, and in bed, there was no other team to face. Just the two of them, utterly focused on performing for each other... or, more than that, on helping each other reach new heights.

"Hnnh," Kevin gasped, breathing out deeply to push past the first few fiery moments.

Jesus, even fingers felt thick after a couple months. His breakup earlier that year had been quick and painless, both of them agreeing that long-distance wasn't their goal... except that he hadn't hooked up since.

Sure, out here there were about a thousand more guys on Grindr and he'd thought about sneaking off to meet a few of them, but he'd always chickened out. It didn't do as much for him as the idea of getting a boyfriend, even if that had been hypothetical until now.

Don't rush things, cowboy. He pulled his attention back to the fingers rubbing deep inside him, igniting nerves he'd almost forgotten about. Well, not like he hadn't pounded himself against a variety of silicone things, but there was nothing like another guy with his eyes fixed on his face or watching his cock twitch.

At fucking *last*, Matty pulled his fingers out with a slow smirk.

Kevin closed his eyes for a minute to pull himself together. He was gonna end up confessing his love—

Fuck. Where had *that* come from?

"You all right?" Matty murmured, his voice cutting through their harsh breathing.

"Good," Kevin instantly whispered back, then grinned. *He doesn't need to know that my heart's on my sleeve or whatever.* "Great," he corrected himself, cracking his eyes.

Matty was just swiping his hand down his cock, the sight of the condom unrolling sending instinctive shudders through Kevin's body.

And then his tip pressed against Kevin's opening, his brown eyes suddenly gentle and warm. They were almost honey-brown with this light and angle.

Kevin was breathless with pleasure as he jerked his head in a quick nod to the unspoken question, and Matty slid on inside.

"Ohhh, yeah," Matty groaned as, inch by inch, he slid inside Kevin's tightness, utterly filling him.

Kevin's whole body throbbed with tight spasms of pleasure and pain, his hands grabbing for Matty's shoulder blades. Those first few seconds were worth it for the quick spike in his arousal.

This was what he'd jerked off to: Matty's muscled arm braced by his face, dark eyes intently focused on his face, the nails of his other hand digging into Kevin's thigh…

And his cock inside Kevin, their breaths almost synchronized as Matty shifted to blanket him again with his weight and dig his knees into the bed.

"Perfect," Kevin moaned, his hands relaxing now to run up and down Matty's back, admiring the strong, smooth planes. God, touching him was heaven. His scent, taste, everything all at once was almost sensory overload.

And then Matty shifted, pushing his cock all the way inside and pulling out again at a slow, measured pace.

"*Yes*," Kevin gasped, the heat building under his stomach again. Now he was raring to go, curling his toes into the bed and arching into Matty as he tried to thrust his hips into him and help out. "Yes, Matty…"

"Fuckin' beautiful," Matty whispered, mouthing at the corner of his jaw, then his earlobe, making Kevin twitch hard with arousal again. "Just gorgeous… Jesus."

Kevin laughed breathlessly. "Yeah. You feel… wow." He gritted his teeth against the words that wanted to spill out. If he started complimenting Matty, he was terrified of how deep those feelings ran.

He just *really* liked the guy. Was turned on by him, even. Every time they were close. Even when they weren't, when he thought about him. They could deal with the rest later.

Matty was moving faster now, pushing in and out with quick thrusts just perfectly angled to make that spot inside him pulse with pleasure. It felt like the base of Kevin's cock was being stroked from inside, and his balls were already tightening with how damn good it was.

How *perfect* it felt.

"Fuck me hard, baby," he breathed out, shuddering again. He needed fast and hard, not slow and sensual.

And Matty obliged, shifting his weight so Kevin's cock no longer got the friction of their bodies, but he could drive in harder instead. Thrust by thrust, Kevin was coming undone, and he was heaving for breath…

"Yes," Matty moaned, mouthing and licking at his neck,

even nipping the skin near his collarbone, then kissing his chin, and his lips, and… he was gonna…

"Ma—hnngh," Kevin moaned into the kiss, his eyes flying open with the *force* of what was about to hit him. Matty swallowed his gasp in hard, rough kisses, his hand palming at the tip of Kevin's cock and jerking up it once, twice, three times—

Kevin was gone, blackness and pleasure and *Matty* all he could think about, rushing through his senses until even the feeling of Matty's bare skin against his was enough to make him twitch hard. In time, even, with the quick clenches and shudders of his body, the warmth squirting from his cock, the way his fingers tingled and clenched rhythmically around Matty's hip and shoulder…

At least Matty pulled back from the kiss slightly to let him gasp for breath, but he kept brushing his lips along Kevin's lightly, thrusting whenever he could. Kevin was squeezing him tight, milking him, clutching him so close he felt like he couldn't tell where either of them ended or began.

"Yes…!" Kevin finally whimpered when he could get a breath, and he was rewarded with the most delicious, growling moan.

His world still spinning, his body still quivering in quick, overwhelmed shudders, Kevin opened his eyes just in time to see Matty's face draw tight. He read his own name on Matty's lips, but Matty didn't have breath or capacity to speak, and his nails were digging hard enough into Kevin's thighs to leave marks.

Fucking *good*. Kevin *wanted* to feel this for days.

When Matty finally settled, thrusting a last few shallow times as his eyelashes fluttered and those dark eyes were looking into his again, Kevin grinned at him, slapping his ass lightly. "Fuckin' eh." His own voice was still breathless.

Matty burst out laughing in quick, silent gasps for breath, and he cupped Kevin's cheek and kissed him hard once again.

This wasn't a *need to fuck you so bad* kiss like it had been some minutes ago.

It was raw emotion spilling over into the only outlet they had, and Kevin knew because it jolted through his body, too —electric, raw, demanding every spare ounce of attention.

Matty was everything to him right now, in a way that was impossible to describe, and he would have given anything not to have Matty slowly pull out of him, but at least he still had him right here in his arms, and…

Shit. Oh, fucking hell, he was falling too hard, too fast.

When Matty left, or got traded, or grew bored, or… or *whatever* would happen, Kevin wasn't gonna be able to handle it. People were gonna know. There was no separating personal and professional anymore, no matter what his buddies had told him.

He rolled his head back against the pillow while Matty slowly drew himself up, rubbing his eyes with his arm.

It took him a few seconds to get his limbs in order again, to uncurl his toes and roll his shoulders to get the sleepiness out of his body.

"God," Matty murmured, as he pulled back and slowly tugged the condom off. "If we wanna do that again, we could always go get tested or whatever." Then, his lips quirked into a quick smile as he eased himself to his feet enough to toss the condom across the room into the waste basket. "Not that that wasn't the best sex I've ever had."

Kevin knew what he meant. "Yeah," he breathed out,

rubbing his arm across his eyes and sitting up. He swung his legs off the edge of the bed, ignoring the burn of pleasure. Scratches and hickeys or not, he was gonna feel this for a couple days, he was certain of it. "Damn it, I still have to sort out my trip home."

That much was true—he had to get his plane ticket, and fuck it, he also needed to go breathe and get out of Matty's air, or he was going to find himself hooked on it. The idea of sleeping curled up in those arms made him simultaneously panic and want to stay.

"Oh, Jesus. Yeah," Matty breathed out, reaching out to punch his shoulder lightly as he sat on the edge of the bed. "God, you'll pay through the nose for tickets now."

"Yeah, I know. Lucky I'm only going to Fredericton," Kevin weakly chuckled.

He pushed through the desire to shove Matty back and sit in his lap, instead getting dressed one piece at a time. "You got your—oh yeah, you're probably driving, huh?"

"Yeah, probably," Matty murmured.

Kevin paused for a second. That reminded him—he had to ask Matty about coming home with him, but doing it now would sound really boyfriend-y, and...

Nah. He'd ask later.

"You're gonna stick around for hockey camp first, right?" Matty asked, yawning as he leaned back on the bed.

Kevin nodded. "Oh yeah, of course. Might take a couple days off the gym and just veg out first. Especially since..." His cheeks were hot.

"Oh, baby." Matty gave him a smirk and pinched his ass before he could jerk away. Kevin laughed and smacked Matty's hand.

The moment of tension had passed, Matty crashing onto

his bed and stretching out on the rumpled sheets while he watched Kevin pull his jeans on. They were back to grinning at each other like buddies.

Who'd just fucked like animals.

"I'll let myself out," Kevin told Matty with a smile, hesitating as he fastened his jeans button and smoothed his shirt down. "Don't strain yourself."

"Okay," Matty laughed, resting his hand behind his head. Which, of course, highlighted his bicep and drew Kevin's eyes to the dark patch of fur under his arm, the way his pecs stretched and rippled…

No, I'm leaving.

"See you," Kevin waved, giving Matty a moment's quick smile before he fled the room and the house.

He walked briskly despite the stinging ache that reminded him how damn much he'd come undone at Matty's hands—how happy he'd been to give in to them.

CHAPTER
Twenty~Seven
MATTY

IT HAD BEEN TWO DAYS SINCE MATTY'S TRULY EPIC SEX WITH Kevin, and two days since they'd talked. He'd been able to wave it off on Sunday, but fuck it, it was Monday now and he was pretty sure this was about the point he was supposed to worry.

He'd sent one *thanks for the great date* good night text after Kevin left and just got a smiley face and *you too* in return, so he hadn't pushed it.

Did Hans get to him? Is he having a gay panic moment?

Matty debated with himself about showing up at his place to make him talk, but he figured he'd wait until Monday and give him some space to deal with everything. Plus, Kevin might legitimately be sleeping all day after prospects camp. It was brutally taxing on the body, after all.

It was weird being back in the arena without any plans to skate, pulling on his jersey but wearing shoes. There were a lot of better-qualified guys who were coaching them on ice. Their job was just motivation. They were talking to the kids, and some other guys were signing autographs or doing skating exercises with them.

This part was the easiest one, but it was kind of scary to think about what they'd say. They'd been coached in it, pulled aside at the end of prospects camp for their workshop in how to motivate young hockey players, but the words still had to be their own.

"Hey."

That was Kevin's voice, and it was warm and resonant.

Matty was already beaming as he turned around, then raised his eyebrows. Kevin already had his jersey on. The dark blue brought out the light blues in his eyes.

"Hey," Matty answered. "You're looking good."

"You, too." Kevin wasn't acting standoffish at all as he came up next to Matty to half-hug him hello. He had that damn addictive spicy musky smell around him again. Must be his aftershave or something.

Matty ran his hand back through his hair and tried not to remember how delicious Kevin tasted, even after that damn garlic butter. "You got something ready? A speech?"

"Yeah. Do you?"

"Something of one. I figured I'd wing it. I'm usually all right at that," Matty admitted.

"Cool," Kevin smiled. "They made it sound pretty informal. And then the Q&A. I wonder what they'll ask?"

"They'll be easier on us than reporters, at least," Matty winked, and Kevin's answering smile made him grin.

"You boys ready?" That was Bryan, the guy in charge of wrangling the volunteers, dipping his head into the locker room.

"Good to go, sir," Kevin answered with a playful salute. "Where are we heading?"

"The kids just had lunch. They're getting excited. You might get swarmed," Bryan warned with a laugh. "They just got done taking selfies with Walker."

"Selfies?" Matty laughed. "They got phones?"

"Some do!" Bryan grinned. "You'd be surprised. Okay, this way." He led them to one of the larger multipurpose rooms.

When they ducked inside, even Matty wasn't expecting the cheer. They weren't the most famous players, either of them, but the kids were already genuinely thrilled that they were there.

And Kevin was beaming, instantly at ease as he waved. "Hey, guys! Wow, there's a lot of you. You all had fun this morning?"

A chorus of eager *yes*es answered the question, and Matty laughed. "Great. What was your favorite bit?"

There were a chorus of answers: skating, drills, and eating.

"Eating?" Matty laughed. "That sounds like me. If you keep going with hockey, be prepared to eat more than you've ever eaten," he winked. "That can be fun, too."

"So, these two are here to talk to you about hockey life," Bryan spoke up from behind them. "You wanna introduce yourselves?"

"Sure." Kevin spoke up before Matty could, already smiling ear to ear. He was so fucking *adorable*. Jesus *Christ*. "I'm Kevin Shaw. I played in New Brunswick last year, and I just got signed for a year to, well..." He gestured at his jersey and laughed. "Which is so, so cool. I'm really looking forward to that! But I think they wanted me there because... well, I'm so handsome," he struck a pose for a second which made the kids laugh and Matty's heart melt into a giant puddle in his chest. "And," he winked, "because I have some pretty recent experience with the lower levels of hockey—AKA, where you guys will start out. Right?"

"Right," a couple kids answered. They were falling for him hook, line, and sinker.

Matty was smiling like an idiot himself, trying not to watch Kevin too much. "And I'm Matty O'Brien. I played for them," he gestured at Kevin's jersey, "before, but I just got called up to the *big* boys' team now," he laughed. "So, yeah. I totally don't sleep with this jersey under my pillow."

The kids laughed for him, too. At least they indulged him with that. Phew.

Matty did pretty damn good, he thought, of winging his speech.

He talked about how hockey could be really hard, but working hard at it was the most important part. After a quick chat about the kinds of things involved in pro hockey training, from gym workouts to nutrition, he explained what he'd always thought about talent. It was cheesy but true—hard work beat talent when talent didn't work hard.

That was when Kevin joined in. "Yeah, I'm the perfect example of that. I'm not really special," he told the kids. "But I got in because I've worked my butt off for years at this, you know? I focused on this all through middle school, high school, university... and eventually they got tired of me and agreed to let me play," he grinned as the kids laughed again.

"And that's the other thing," Kevin added. "It's a career, you know? But it isn't easy. So, you can't just focus on hockey being the only thing in your life. Make sure you study hard in school and come up with a backup plan. Maybe you don't mind teaching, or science, or being a nurse, or... whatever. There's tons and tons of awesome things to do. You gotta make sure you're not locking yourself in."

"And focus on your friends and family, too," Matty smiled. God, they were all watching so intently. There was a blond kid near the front who looked like he was about to start taking notes.

"That's right," Kevin agreed. "And eventually, boyfriends or girlfriends," he grinned at them.

That got another laugh, along with some giggling and "ew"s from the kids.

"I know, I know. But the people around you will be working hard to help you succeed, too, so… you know, be great to them," Kevin smiled. "And make sure they're great for you. Make hockey not the *only* thing you eat, sleep, and breathe. Make it part of a big, exciting life. There's a thousand other things you can do along with hockey. Don't miss out on that."

A chill ran down Matty's spine at the simple, yet expressive words.

Part of a big, exciting life.

Shit, Kevin was a natural-born leader… maybe captain material. He'd never seen him like this—never had the chance to yet—but it made Matty fall in love with him just that little bit more. Plus, Kevin was totally being dad material right now.

Fuck's sakes. Too. Soon.

The kids were starting to ask questions, so Matty focused on them again. He had hours and hours to think about Kevin, but only an hour with these kids. They deserved his full attention, or as much of it as he could spare when Kevin wasn't flashing that huge, eager smile.

CHAPTER
Twenty-Eight
KEVIN

Somehow, in talking to Bryan about the kids' hockey camp and meeting a couple of the guys in the hallway who were on their way to help coach, Kevin got separated from Matty after they were done talking to the kids.

He did spot Matty hesitating by the locker room door for a minute, but he couldn't extricate himself from the conversation about practice schedules without being rude. And then Matty got shy, or nervous, or something, and ducked out before Kevin could catch him.

It was on his mind for a little while on the way home, and he kept fidgeting with his phone. Should he call him up? Hang out tonight, now that their big commitment was done? But they were each about to head home again, taking advantage of these last few intermittent weeks before the 24/7 hockey life began.

Was now the best time to talk to Matty?

The thought of what he had to do first distracted him from that question.

He couldn't keep living in fear that Matty would show up at his place at the same time Hans was home.

In fact, it was great timing that he ran into Hans hanging out with a couple other guys outside the arena.

And *excellent* timing that Hans was just saying, "...course Kevin signed up to volunteer with Matty."

"Why's that?" Kevin asked casually, letting the steel arena side door slam shut behind him as he tucked his hands in his jeans pockets, approaching the group.

He noted the other guys awkwardly shifting and chuckling, but he didn't give a fuck who they were or why they were talking to Hans. His gaze was locked on his roommate.

Hans shifted and licked his lips, his eyes cutting to the side door and then back to Kevin. "Nothing."

"No, I wanna know. You've been talking a lot about me lately, I heard." Kevin forced himself to keep his voice friendly. This wasn't gonna become a brawl in the parking lot, by any means. He just had to talk things through.

Hans straightened up, pushing himself away from the side of the building. "You know, just seems like you guys are… pretty tight."

"Yeah?" Kevin asked. "Why's that?"

"Always meeting up, making sure you leave separately… working out together… you know."

"And that's different from Fisher and CJ how?" Kevin asked. "Or any one of… shit, how many dozens of guys are buddies around here?"

"Right, right," Hans answered, but his voice was not in the slightest convinced.

Kevin paused for long moments, his eyes flickering between Hans's. Hans looked guilty when he scrutinized him, but he stood his ground. Kevin jerked his chin up slightly, keeping his voice down. "I don't care if you think or say I'm gay to anyone and everyone. It's not something to be ashamed about, and it's really none of your business anyway. Just don't sabotage my fuckin' career and we're good."

He held Hans's gaze for half a second, then turned on his heel and strode off for the bus stop.

What he didn't expect was the crunch of footsteps behind him. A wild part of him, born and bred in a place where guys had fucked him up for even admitting he *could* be gay, tensed up and planned where to grab Hans's arm and throw him to the concrete, but Hans didn't touch him. He just caught up beside him.

"I'm sorry."

That made Kevin stop in his tracks. He examined Hans's face for a second or two, his brows drawing together. That was an awfully fast apology.

"Yeah?" he responded carefully, turning again to walk towards the bus stop. He walked slower this time, making it clear Hans could follow.

And follow Hans did, keeping him company towards the bus. "Yeah. I, uh… I got… wrapped up in losing my spot. Maybe forever."

There was no mistaking the raw emotion in his voice, even if Hans tried to flatten it out and sound casual.

Kevin believed him now. He nodded slightly, scuffing down the street toward the shelter. "That's gotta suck. But man, I offered to train with you. I could've—*can*—help."

He wasn't sure he'd trust Hans again soon, but he had to live with the guy for now.

Hans hesitated, then shook his head. "No, you don't need to do that."

"Either way, *you* do. That's the difference right now,"

Kevin told him. No better time than the present for brutal honesty. "You have to work harder, or you *are* gonna lose that spot forever."

Hans's eyes steeled for a second, and it seemed almost like he might shove Kevin, but he held back. "What?"

"I just told the kids, I'm not that talented," Kevin laughed. "I'm not some wonder kid. Jesus, I just got my bachelors degree."

Hans conceded that with a slight smile and nod.

"I just work really fuckin' hard at what I do. So a little tough love: work harder, and work more. Then it'll be a fair fight for my position, right?"

They were at the bus stop, and Hans was slowly settling down again, his shoulders sinking. "Yeah. Uh, you… you gonna stay living with me after…?"

"Depends," Kevin told him, keeping his voice calm. As much as he wanted to punch Hans for being a dick, that wouldn't solve much. "You gonna be a dick every time I have a buddy over? Or, if it came to it, a boyfriend?"

Hans flinched and winced, but he looked down the street for a second, sucking on his teeth. Then he looked back at Kevin and shook his head. "I'll mind my own business. Uh, you might wanna know this." It was almost painful for him to speak, so Kevin waited it out. "The other guys told me straight-up… it'd be awesome if you *were* gay."

Kevin quirked his brow.

"They all want to support whoever the first guy to come out is." Hans cracked a small smile, and Kevin knew the look of a man trying his damnedest to accept defeat gracefully.

Kevin smiled back, then nodded. "Here's the bus. You coming home?"

"Nah. I think I'm gonna walk around a bit," Hans admitted. "Clear my head."

Kevin hesitated as the bus pulled to a stop by them, then offered his hand. When Hans took it, they shook. It was a tentative trust between them, and Hans still looked like he was worried the gay would rub off on him, but it was better now.

"See you later."

"See ya." Hans turned to walk down the street, hands in his pockets.

Just as well, because Kevin wasn't heading home.

Walking up to Hans had been a piece of cake. He hadn't even had to make his message sink home with knuckles or threats.

Approaching Matty's door? Jesus, that was like slogging through molasses.

Kevin felt a little shitty for ignoring Matty yesterday and today, for not once bringing up the fact that he *was* really happy with the way the date had gone and that he wanted more like that.

It hadn't taken long—just long enough to book his flight and arrange for a ride from the airport—before he'd regretted leaving Matty's house. Especially before he told Matty what was really on his mind.

Whatever Matty wanted to be, he wanted from him. Thing was, he was gonna have to ask for it. They couldn't keep making out, hooking up, and fucking fleeing. No, *he* couldn't keep doing that. It wasn't Matty running away every time, after all.

He sucked on his lower lip for a second, then let out a slow, shaky breath and walked up the porch steps.

It wasn't like he couldn't just greet Matty as a buddy, walk in and hang out with him, but… Matty deserved better than that. Matty was just waiting for him to man up, and he was here to do that.

A few moments after he rang the bell, he heard voices inside and his stomach jolted with nerves.

Then, Matty was beaming at him, pushing open the screen door for him. "Hey, man. I was gonna wait but you looked pretty caught up."

Kevin jerked his head in a nod and stepped into the foyer.

A glance at the living room beyond showed him CJ, Chris, and Fisher. The usual guys, then. The ones Matty kept telling him he didn't care if they found out.

Thank God.

"Yeah, no problem. Uh, before anything, I just gotta… You wanna come home with me? Visit Cam and hang out with me properly—no, I mean, *date* me properly, away from the gym and Hans and all this bullshit, and…"

He was positive his cheeks were tomato-red, but the words spilled from his lips, not at all in the suave order he'd imagined them into on the bus. "I mean, as, not just buddies," he desperately started to clarify. "Like, boyfriends? Do you do boyfriends? I do boyfriends, but I never asked—"

Shit, was he supposed to do this in front of his friends? Should he have texted? He definitely should have texted.

Matty was grinning, pulling him in by the waist in one hard, fast jerk.

Kevin stumbled into Matty's body, barely getting his arms around Matty's shoulders as Matty kissed him hard.

Oh, God, it was like coming home into Matty's arms. He

hadn't realized until this second how much he'd missed those full lips, those warm eyes, the strong hands on him…

Especially the warm lips that slid along his own for a second or two as Matty tilted his head so they could kiss deeper and Kevin's hands finally settled on Matty's waist, curling in to grip and claim him every bit as much as Matty was staking his own claim.

Even a couple days of avoiding Matty had him feeling like he'd never breathed air before when he pulled back.

And then he realized there was a mix of groans, whoops, and laughter from the living room.

Kevin wanted to melt through the floor instead of look at them, but Matty was grinning broadly at him.

"I've never been wooed so hard in my life," Matty teased, dark eyes sparkling with mischief. "What a romantic."

Kevin covered his face with both hands now, letting go of Matty. "Shit."

They were all laughing now, even him.

When he managed to drag his hands down his face, Matty's hand curled around his wrist to help pull his hands down, then slipped into his own as Matty pulled him into the living room.

"Fredericton. What a romantic invitation." CJ was grinning from the armchair, his feet on the coffee table.

"Fuck Paris," Fisher agreed. "Someone take me to Fredericton."

"I would if you spoke any French," CJ shook his head.

"Damn it. I missed my chance," Fisher dramatically groaned.

Kevin realized he hadn't really been breathing, still too wound-up to make any eye contact, but as he gradually relaxed, he started to laugh along with them again.

They were being teased, but it was friendly. Just like his buddies back home would have done—making fun of him, but not because they wanted him to feel that guilty squirm like he was doing something wrong.

No—because they wanted him to look embarrassed.

"Fuck off," Kevin laughed, which started another round of laughter.

Matty pulled Kevin over to the couch. "Guess we better book me a ticket. What flight are you on?"

Kevin rubbed his face before he pulled out his phone, his head still spinning at how fast everything had happened.

All he'd had to do all this time was ask. Maybe not like a backcountry bumpkin who'd never been kissed, but he could live that down.

Maybe, eventually.

He had the feeling these guys wouldn't let that happen for a while, but that was surprisingly okay with him.

CHAPTER

Twenty~Nine

MATTY

IF ONLY MATTY DIDN'T HAVE THE SHITTIEST TIMING IN THE world, he'd feel like the luckiest guy in the world.

As it was, he'd been stuck in his goddamn tiny hometown for a week now, and the itch under his skin to get out of his fucking hometown had just hit critical at a dinner conversation about why he wasn't dating some hot Toronto chick. The whole time, he'd been thinking about how soft Kevin's skin was.

Sometimes thinking about how damn gay he was made Matty laugh; other times, it twisted the knot in his chest until he itched to break and blurt it out over supper.

When he and Kevin had agreed to be boyfriends, they hadn't really had the chance to discuss *this* yet. He knew Kevin planned to tell his buddies and family about him sometime, because there was no way they could hide this when he was going out to Fredericton to visit everyone with him, but...

His own family was different.

He rubbed a hand down his face as he packed up his bag.

He loved his parents, most of the time, but a week at a time was about all he could stand.

It was a damn good thing he had to fly out of Toronto tomorrow, and he had a good excuse: seeing some old *and* new buddies in the same place.

His family understood. After all, they could get him wanting to be close to his hockey buddies. Matty just wasn't sure they'd understand if he was also boning one of them.

He thought he'd done pretty damn well explaining away his daily Skype calls to Kevin, distracting himself reading breakdowns of the upcoming season and how good (or bad, according to some commentators) his chances were, and going for long walks with Jasmine.

Sometimes all-day walks, but hey, whatever worked.

But he wasn't about to whine about it. His family *probably* wouldn't hate him. They'd just… do that subtle thing, which was worse.

He loaded his pack in the car, hugged his parents good-bye, got Jasmine settled in the passenger seat, and got the fuck out of Dodge.

Passing city limits was the second-best part of his day.

The best? Pulling over to read a text—not from Kevin, which would normally be the highlight of his day, but from Chris.

Nate texted. He hasn't been around cause he has a girlfriend now. He's moving out. Know anyone who needs a new roommate? ;)

When the meaning sank in, Matty gasped so sharply Jasmine whined and looked over at him. He almost flung his phone at the dashboard in excitement.

"Okay, girl," he told her. "I hope you're ready to fly to a tiny little place that's a little less shitty than that place was.

And then ask my boyfriend if he'll move in, before we've even twice—wait, I don't need to tell *you* that. That's not appropriate for doggy ears."

Jasmine eagerly wagged her tail, trying to squirm over to get her nose into his lap.

He laughed and pushed her back gently, scratching her ears there instead. "No trying to drive. You need a walk before we finish the drive? Let's go."

Tomorrow's trip was a lot more exciting than this one had been. He'd be with Kevin 24/7 for this week in Cam's guest room, where Kevin was staying to spread around the burden of hosting him each time he visited.

By the time he got back to the car, Matty was calm enough to text back.

Thanks man. I'll ask him when I see him :)

Finally, just tomorrow, they could be alone together. Well, not quite alone, but away from anyone who would judge them.

Kevin wasn't surprised to get a call from Cam that evening while he was trying to figure out what to pack to impress Matty and also be comfortable that week.

"Hey, man."

"Dude, you're flying in tomorrow!" was Cam's excitable greeting.

Matty laughed. "Yeah, I know I am."

"Bro. It's been too long."

"Brooo," Matty snickered, grabbing another Henley t-shirt to shove into the bag. "Yeah, it's been way too long. We just never made it out, huh?"

"Good of you to come back and see me." Cam's voice was light, almost teasing, and Matty hesitated for half a second. But he couldn't come out to Cam without asking Kevin's permission first, could he?

"Yeah. You were my best bud out here for ages."

"Kevin's really glad to have you around." Cam was speaking more seriously now, but then he chuckled. "And he's cool to hang around, huh?"

"Yeah, he's awesome," Matty agreed lightheartedly. "Thanks for letting me crash, especially with Jazz."

"No problem! Noah's been bugging me for months now to get a dog, anyway," Cam laughed. "He loves having 'em around."

"Awesome," Matty laughed.

"Kevin likes 'em, too, doesn't he?"

Matty blushed as he shoved another pair of jeans into his bag. If he didn't know better, he'd swear Cam already knew. "Yeah, he's great with her." He rifled through the hangers, choosing a couple more things.

"Good," Cam approved. He paused for a few seconds, then laughed. "You only packing now?"

"I just got back from home," Matty complained, rolling his eyes. "Shut up."

"Ah, right, yeah," Cam answered. "How was that?"

Matty grunted. "Not the best visit, but it was just long enough."

"Yeah," Cam murmured. "Folks got you drove?"

Matty blew a quick sigh out through pursed lips. "Just about drove nuts, yeah. All the *why aren't you dating some Toronto girl yet—*"

Shit. Wait.

Cam was gay, and he was gay, but they hadn't actually

talked about it. Hell, Matty hadn't even known for certain Cam *was* gay, except that weird thing with his shitty ex who'd dumped him in the ambulance on the way to hospital. Well, and then he'd gotten a boyfriend within days of getting back home, which Matty had endlessly teased him about.

"They really leaning on you? Shit," Cam groaned. "That sucks. Don't worry, man. We're cooler out here."

"Yeah, good," Matty laughed. "Okay, I gotta finish packing and get Jasmine's food ready."

"Okay!" Cam brightly added. "See you tomorrow, man."

Matty had only just put his phone down when it buzzed with a text—from Cam, no less. That was kinda weird.

He picked it up, then squinted. It was a screenshot of a phone conversation, but only a picture text and its original sender—Fisher—was visible.

The photo was Matty himself with his arm around Kevin's shoulder, and Matty was looking goddamn starstruck or some shit as he watched Kevin.

It took him a second to place it. That had been when they were booking these plane tickets, right after Kevin's incredibly adorable flustered proposal on the doorstep.

Matty's cheeks flushed with heat as he slapped his phone against his forehead. Cam had been playing with him after all.

He rolled his eyes, even though he was laughing. Goddamn his buddies. "Fuck you, Fisher!" he called out, knowing Fisher would hear from the kitchen.

He heard a burst of laughter in return. "Yeah, you wish!"

Matty groaned and sent a quick, *Fucking Fisher* back to Cam, but he was still laughing as he zipped up his bag.

CHAPTER

Thirty

KEVIN

"You look like you're about to twitch out of your skin," Cam laughed at Kevin. "Relax, man."

Kevin was staring out the airport window past the luggage belt. He knew they had to stick around until the guys unloaded Matty's dog, too, but he was so eager to at least see him.

It was gonna be a full car load with him, Cam, Floyd, Matty, and then Matty's dog, but Cam was driving and Floyd had insisted on coming along to see him. It was fair enough, since Floyd was probably Kevin's other closest friend. Well, there was Ryan, too, but Ryan was on a building site for another twenty minutes. Floyd had wanted the news from the horse's mouth.

Even if it was a little late for that.

Kevin had turned about five shades of red, according to Cam, when Cam showed him the photo text from Fisher. It wasn't like he could keep it a secret after that, and he *had* laughed at Cam teasing Matty on the phone last night about it.

God, a week apart from him was stifling. This season was gonna be brutal, but Kevin had managed to put all that out of his mind for now.

The stairs had just been rolled up to the plane, and people were starting to leave.

Oh, God, it was impossible to miss Matty's rolling walk as he trotted down the stairs, then stopped to ask a ramp worker something, jerking his thumb toward the plane. Then he beamed and nodded, raising a hand in a quick salute before turning to the terminal building.

Kevin headed right up past the luggage belt to the entry doors, tuning out Cam and Floyd entirely as he watched Matty approach. At the last second, just before he walked through the door, Matty noticed him, too.

The way his face lit up, his face splitting in a grin, his body jolting to attention as he stood straighter…

Kevin didn't give a fuck who else was around and watching them; he grabbed Matty and kissed him the moment he walked through the door, and Matty's strong arms were hugging him close to him at the same moment.

He made himself pull back after a couple seconds, fully aware that it was hard to kiss while grinning so much. "Hey."

"Hey," Matty answered, sounding breathless. He kept his hand on Kevin's arm, which made Kevin tingle with pleasure. "That was some *hello* there."

"Hope you don't mind if we don't say hi like that," Floyd cracked a joke from behind them.

Matty and Kevin both laughed, and Kevin kept hold of Matty's hand as they turned. Matty leaned in for half-hugs with both Floyd and Cam.

"Thanks for picking me up. Jesus, I got a whole welcoming committee."

"Couldn't leave 'em behind," Kevin rolled his eyes. "Everyone else is back at Cam's place starting up the barbecue."

"Awesome!" Matty exclaimed. "Should've come to visit months ago."

"Yeah, asshole," Cam exclaimed, punching his arm as they wandered to the baggage carousel. "And yet Kevin shows up and suddenly you're flying here, *with* your dog..."

Matty's face crinkled sheepishly as he laughed. "Hey, you didn't come out and see us, either."

"Fair, I guess," Cam snorted. "Still."

Then, Matty grabbed Kevin's arm with his spare hand, his eyes alight with some kind of news. His words were spilling out of him almost faster than his lips could move. And given what Kevin knew about his lips' capabilities, that was pretty impressive.

"Dude. Dude, my other roommate, the one you never met 'cause he's never home, Nate? He's moving out. So Chris texted and, like, I dunno, you were saying yesterday Hans has gotten better, but if you wanted to move in, bro, you could totally, like, move in."

This must have been what Kevin looked like a week or so ago. He couldn't stop himself laughing first, then shaking his head quickly when Matty started to look dismayed. "I'm not laughing at the idea, I'm—man, I'm rubbing off on you."

"Gross, we don't need to hear that kind of talk," Floyd teased.

"Shut up, Mr. *I'm just gonna be with my boyfriend 24/7 now*," Kevin laughed, and Matty laughed, too.

Then, Kevin could turn his attention back to Matty.

"That's so romantic," Kevin teased, but there was no denying it. Hans *had* gotten better over the last week, but living with him? For a year? He wasn't Hans's fucking enlightenment project.

And yeah, it was slightly weird to move in with the guy he'd just started dating, but there was no *way* he could turn down that opportunity. Chris, CJ, and Fisher seemed like the best roommates, and he'd have his own room anyway. Though, he suspected he wouldn't be spending a lot of time in it.

"Yeah," Kevin nodded after a second of thought. "I'd like that."

Matty beamed. "It's settled. I'll get Chris to text you all the lease and bill stuff."

"Awesome," Kevin smiled.

"I think they moved faster than any of us," Cam marveled from behind them.

Kevin turned red. Yeah, it *did* come off as a bit fast, but…

"Okay, Jasmine's supposed to be ready now over there, so I'll just go pick her up and be back for the luggage—"

Matty strode off, almost turning the wrong way before he found the right way and strode off about as fast as his legs would carry him. He was still beet-red.

Kevin couldn't stop laughing under his breath as he waited by the baggage carousel. Matty was on fire with energy. He looked like he would walk clear to town if they let him.

To be fair, Kevin felt the exact same.

Their only interruption was on the way out of the airport, after Matty had Jasmine's kennel loaded onto a trolley and his suitcase on top of it, and a couple guys stopped them.

"Hey, are you… Matty…?"

"Yeah," Matty answered, eyes flickering between them both before he smiled. "Hockey fan?"

"Shit, it *is* you. Sorry, I thought we were just gonna freak out some stranger," one of the guys laughed, shaking hands. "Do you mind if we get a photo?"

Matty was turning pink as the rest of them grinned, but he shrugged. "Yeah, of course."

Kevin smirked. "Want me to take a photo?"

The guys were watching him, looking at each other like they weren't quite sure.

"This is Kevin. He's only just got drafted. And that's Cam Riley, of course."

The guys both looked young, university-aged. One of them was being pretty cool and looking embarrassed, but the other guy's eyes widened. "Oh, that's—wow, I thought so, but I didn't wanna, like… assume. That's awesome. Man, could I get a photo?"

Cam laughed and grabbed Kevin to steer him into the shot. They all grinned for the camera.

They had a couple minutes' conversation about the Toronto teams' chances this year before the embarrassed-looking guy tried to steer his friend off.

But the other guy was determined to get in a word. "So, uh, that article... I guess it's true?"

Kevin's stomach sank. "What article?"

"The one... *oh*, you might have been on the plane."

"It's nothing," the other guy tried to say, but Matty shook his head.

"No, I wanna know." Matty slid out his phone and Kevin did the same, turning off airplane mode.

"Um, some journalist in Toronto... dug up a couple things... a photo, and stuff..."

Oh, shit. Kevin swapped a quick look with Matty, then looked back at their fan. "What's your name, dude?"

"B-Brian." Brian held his ground, despite how nervous as he looked. "I mean, I don't mind, it's none of my business, but... it's a pretty big deal. They're saying you're dating."

Kevin tried not to remember his media training and not react to that. "Yeah? Are we in Weekly World News or something?"

"Just a couple sports sites, and Twitter, and a Reddit feed, and..." the guy trailed off, clearing his throat.

Kevin's face burned as his phone started to vibrate almost constantly in his hand, alert after alert hitting him. He took a quick glance down at his phone, then offered a tight smile to Brian. "Thanks for the heads-up. I better call my agent now. Good meeting you two."

Matty shook hands with them both and steered them off while Cam and Floyd closed in around them, leaning over their shoulders for a look at their phones.

"Oh, boy," Cam breathed out, pulling out his own and showing the rest of them.

Kevin and Matty sitting in a tree?

There was a blurry photo from across the arena of the two of them sitting in the bleachers, but it was impossible to make out the facial details—thank God. But it definitely looked like them.

Cam turned the phone towards himself and skimmed the article. "Who's the asshole talking to the press? Someone confirmed you're together."

"Two guesses, and the first doesn't count," Matty muttered.

Kevin felt like an idiot for not just punching Hans the

first time around. "Well," Kevin murmured, swapping looks with Matty. "This is gonna be a thing."

Only once they were in the car, the kennel in the back with the suitcase, Jasmine sprawled in the middle of the backseat while Floyd sat up front with Cam, leaving the backseat for the lovers, did Floyd speak up.

"You guys worried about that, at all, or…?"

Matty shook his head slowly, though Kevin's heart still instinctively sank with worry. "No," Matty reflected. "We can get away with a ridiculous amount of PDA just from being… hockey buddies. I mean, a lot of guys go a pretty long way to be gay and people still think they're joking around."

Kevin laughed. That much was true, if he thought about it. "Sort of an open secret." He could live with that. The headlines would die down, maybe. He could call his agent later and ask if he could just be vague about rumors for a while.

He glanced down at his phone. It was Fisher.

Want me to beat the shit out of him?? I'm on my way.

Kevin laughed under his breath and showed Matty the text, then settled back to answer.

Nah man. Let him torpedo himself. I won't be around him much longer.

You moving in???

Yeah :)

Fucking awesome. Welcome bro.

Thanks! See you soon.

Kevin smiled and pocketed his phone, then looked back at Matty.

"And if we decide we wanna take advantage of this and be the poster boys, we'll figure that out later," Matty nodded, even though he looked nervous. "Now, what's for supper?"

"Dude, you two are *boyfriends* as of, what, last week? And now you're moving in?"

Ryan had just gotten here, his clothing still covered in sawdust, and he was trying to awkwardly avoid standing too close to the bee hives tucked into the corner of the brothers' yards. Cam and his two brothers, Jackson and Thomas, and now all three of their boyfriends, shared one huge communal backyard space.

Most recently, Cam had put in a couple bee hives, and everyone was enjoying it. Except Ryan, when he came straight from work and the bees tried to gather sawdust from his clothes, thinking it to be pollen.

He gently brushed another couple bees off him, then shrugged off his outer shirt and left it on the grass. "They can harvest it or whatever."

Kevin laughed, stretching his legs out from the chair on the porch. "Yeah, you know how it goes."

"And what about Fredericton? The offer?"

That was Cam, his eyes bright and curious as he glanced between them.

"I don't think that was legit," Matty murmured. "I'm pretty sure that was a journalist. My agent never heard from anyone."

"Oh, shit," Cam muttered. "Of course. What an asshole."

"But trades, legit trades, we can't control," Kevin spoke up. "Not really. We'll move where we have to."

Matty nodded, and he reached out to rest a hand on the plastic arm of Kevin's chair.

Kevin put his own hand over it, well aware of the group of guys watching them both. Alex and Thomas were sitting together on the porch swing, while Chase perched on the table next to Jackson, who manned the grill. Noah was playing with Jasmine, stretched out on the grass while she tried to paw at him to play. Cam was near the hives, watching the bees work on harvesting the sawdust from Ryan's jacket.

"If that happens, or one of us gets cut, we'll just figure it out," Kevin quietly said.

All of them were smiling like Kevin had just figured out the secret to life, and Matty, most importantly, was beaming at him.

It was the conversation they hadn't really properly had yet, and it was all happening so simply. Despite Kevin's layers of worry, it really *could* be that simple.

They could figure shit out as they went.

They didn't have to have the answers now. That even went for Matty's shitty family, whom he'd tried to avoid talking about on Skype, but Kevin had picked up on right away. And they'd deal with Hans when they got back to Toronto. All Kevin had to do was move out, and probably stop their friends from taking Hans out back for a kicking.

One thing at a time, and this barbecue was just about smelling ready.

Epilogue

MATTY

THE GUEST BEDROOM AT CAM'S PLACE HAD A PERFECTLY comfortable bed, but what made it perfect was that it already smelled like Kevin after a week of him staying in it.

Jasmine was settled downstairs for the night, more than happy with the nest of blankets Noah had made for her and the treats he'd snuck her. After the barbecue, which had stretched on for a good couple hours, they'd finally drifted apart—the brothers and plus-ones to their own houses, Ryan and Floyd back to their own places.

And now, at last, Matty was more or less alone with Kevin. He'd expected the moment to be a lot steamier than it was, but despite how on-edge he was, it just felt kinda weird to mess around in their friends' room.

And now that Kevin was gonna be moving in with him at the beginning of next month, they were about to have a whole lot of time around each other.

So, instead, Matty held up the cover for Kevin to crawl under, then snaked an arm around his shoulder to pull him in nice and close.

Kevin fit perfectly against him, that hard little body nestling against his side. Kevin's hand rested on his stomach, his other arm curled awkwardly under his head.

They laughed as they found different positions to shift into, slowly finding one that was comfortable for them both and wouldn't break their necks by morning.

"It's… really nice to be out here," Matty admitted quietly. Everyone had been so damn welcoming, even though he'd hardly known the brothers except for Cam.

And Kevin looked so happy and comfortable around them, just as Matty felt around his own buddies. Hopefully vice versa now, too, as they grew acquainted with each others' friends.

"Man, it's killing me not just… crawling all over you right now," Kevin murmured, his voice husky as he rubbed Matty's arm, but it wasn't necessarily a come-on.

Matty teased back, "We've got a week out here, bro." A whole glorious week to themselves, out in almost the middle of nowhere, with a bunch of friends. "Accidents will happen."

"I hope they do," Kevin snickered, settling his head against Matty's shoulder. His breathing was already even and deep. "I was *almost* desperate enough to ask for Skype sex, you know."

Matty laughed deeply. "I'm pretty sure we'll get the chance to get good at that."

Kevin hummed, the vibration traveling through Matty's shoulder and chest. "About that… you were cool with that, earlier? Just figuring this shit out later? I mean, that's what boyfriends do."

"Mmhmm," Matty nodded slightly, stroking Kevin's hair for a second. As he fidgeted with it, he gazed into those baby blue eyes that were so earnestly searching his own.

"September's gonna get rough, but we'll plan carefully is all."

Kevin nodded, too. "And living together will make it a lot easier."

That made Matty glow all over again. "I'm glad that didn't freak you out. I just got excited."

"Me, too," Kevin admitted. "Hans is a real dick."

"He is." Matty scowled, pressing his lips into Kevin's hair. "As for moving in. I… I don't know if it's too early…"

"We've known each other a while now," Kevin laughed under his breath, but he was shifting to look expectantly at him.

That meant he knew what was coming.

"I love you," Matty murmured. "It sounds stupid, but I can't explain it. It just… happened."

"Nah, man. It's not at all," Kevin told him with a quick shake of his head, propping himself up on his elbow. "That's what people always say happens. You just *know*. And I've known for a while that I love you, too. So, I might be stupid, too," he laughed breathily.

"So," Matty echoed, his smile growing. "Cool. We'll both be stupid together, then." He tilted his head back and Kevin took the invitation, leaning down for a long, slow kiss before they settled down together again.

They had so much to talk about that Matty felt like he could chat for hours, but he was already getting so sleepy. Just having Kevin here, nestled into his arm, was enough to wash away all traces of his stresses over the last couple weeks.

As his eyelids grew heavy, Kevin went quiet, too. The last thing Matty remembered thinking before sleep made him smile faintly.

We're the slowest-moving fastest-moving couple I know.

They were a couple now. Somehow, where he'd least expected it, Matty had just stumbled into the arms of this man. No matter how long it had taken them to figure it out, he was lucky beyond belief.

Hockey had brought them together, but it wasn't everything… it was just the beginning of their big, exciting lives together.

Grind (The Riley Brothers #6)

"I CAN'T KEEP IT PROFESSIONAL. NOT WITH YOU."

James is glad to pay the price of starting a new life, even if his family turned their backs on him when he transitioned. He's starting a business with his hunky carpenter friend to pay off his medical debt. But what if Ryan is the only one to see past it all and love him inside and out?

Ryan is hard to rattle. When he knows what he wants, nothing can stop him. Clever, caring, bossy new partner James has won Ryan's heart, and he doesn't back down from a challenge—or even threats.

They both know mixing business with pleasure is a bad idea, but the pull between them is too hard to resist. Can James let Ryan in, and can Ryan have it all with the one who's won his heart?

Grind is the sixth book in The Riley Brothers, a low-angst series filled with brotherly banter and small-town smiles. This steamy, standalone gay romance novel can be enjoyed on its own, and promises a happily-ever-after ending.

Grind

Brooklyn Boys:

Electric Sunshine

Live Wire

Boiling Point

F-Word:

Flaunt

Freak

Faux

Forever

Freedom

After:

Afterburn

Afterglow

Aftermath

Shared Universes:

Shelter

Adore

Miracle

Redemption

Limelight

Barely Regal